MW01058581

SLOW TRAINS OVERHEAD

OTHER BOOKS BY REGINALD GIBBONS

POETRY

Roofs, Rivers, Roads
The Ruined Motel
Saints
Maybe It Was So
Sparrow: New and Selected Poems
Homage to Longshot O'Leary
It's Time
In the Warhouse (chapbook)
Fern-Texts (chapbook)
Creatures of a Day

TRANSLATION

Selected Poems of Luis Cernuda
Guillén on Guillén: The Poetry and the Poet (with A. L. Geist)
Euripides, *Bakkhai* (with Charles Segal)
Sophocles, *Antigone* (with Charles Segal)
Sophocles, *Selected Poems: Odes and Fragments*

FICTION

Five Pears or Peaches
Sweetbitter

Men and women obscure in their labor.   BARACK OBAMA

CONTENTS

ACKNOWLEDGMENTS

These works were first published in, or have been selected from, the following books and periodicals:

"A Large Heavy-Faced Woman, Pocked, Unkempt, in a Loose Dress," *Saints* (Persea Books, 1986)

"Five Pears or Peaches," "Forsaken in the City," "Friday Snow," "Mekong Restaurant," "Mission," "No Matter What Has Happened This May," "On Belmont," "The Vanishing Point," *Five Pears or Peaches* (Broken Moon Press, 1991)

"Hungry Man Raids Supermarket," *Maybe It Was So* (University of Chicago Press, 1991)

"Admiration," "City," "Elsewhere Children," "Sparrow," "The Affect of Elms," "The Blue Dress," *Sparrow: New and Selected Poems* (LSU Press, 1997)

"A Meeting," "Boy on a Busy Corner," *Homage to Longshot O'Leary* (Holy Cow! Press, 1999)

"A Leap," "Avian Time" (from "Avian Migrations"), "Oh," *It's Time* (LSU Press, 2002)

"An Aching Young Man," "Celebration," "Enough," "Ode: At a Twenty-Four-Hour Gas Station," "Ode: Citizens," "On Sad Suburban Afternoons of Autumn," "Rich Pale Pink," "Adams & Wabash" (as "Where moon light angles through"), *Creatures of a Day* (LSU Press, 2008)

"A Man in a Suit," *North American Review* (1995)

"Christmas" (as "Christmas in Juvenile Court"), *Creative Nonfiction* (1997)

"Nonna," *Chicago Tribune Magazine* (1991)

"Slow Motion," *Harper's* (1993)

ADAMS & WABASH

Where moon light angles
           through the east-west streets,
down among the old-
           for-America
tall buildings that changed
           the streets of other
cities, circulate
           elevated trains
overhead, shrieking
           and drumming, lit by
explosions of sparks
           that harm no one, and
the shadowed persons
           walking underneath
the erratic waves—
           not of the lake but
of noise—move through fog
           sieved by the steel mesh
of the supporting
           structures or through rain
that rinses pavements
           and the el platforms
or through new snow that
           quiets corners, moods,
riveted careers.
           Working for others
with hands, backs, machines,
           men built hard towers
that part the high air;
           women and men built,
cooked, cleaned, delivered,
           typed and filed, carried
and delivered, priced
           and sold. The river
and air were filthy.
           In a hundred years

builders would migrate
                north a mile but in
those modern times this
                was all the downtown
that was. And circling
                on a round-cornered
rectangle of tracks
                run the trains, clockwise
and counter, veering
                through or loop-the-loop
and out again. Why
                even try to list
the kinds of places
                men and women made
to make money? Not
                enough of them, yet
too many. From slow
                trains overhead some
passengers can still
                see stone ornaments,
pilasters, lintels,
                carved by grandfathers,
great uncles, and gone
                second cousins of
today—gargoyle heads
                and curving leaves, like
memorials for
                that which was built to
be torn down again
                someday, for those who
got good wages out
                of all this building
or were broken by
                it, or both, yet whose
labor preserves a
                record of labor,
imagination,
                ambition, skill, greed,

folly, courage, cost,
               error, story, so
that a time before
               remains present with-
in the dark spark-lit
               loud careening now.

A MEETING

While the unaware world is both opening and closing toward our future
on this night of sparkling gusts and frozen pavements,
inside a large shabby upstairs room
thirty or so are gathered to honor the undaunted
long-lived hero
(while she thinks of her secret despair from time to time, of retreats she did
    not let others see, of rising again and again in the teeth of cold winds,
    of the campaign that is about to begin),
to praise her resolve and stamina
(which she has maintained thanks to her mother's love or her father's, when
    she was young;
or despite their indifference, but because of the love, when she was young,
    of some teacher or aunt who opened a way for her, and whom she
    cannot thank now because the years have closed behind her),

and we all sit together on folding chairs arranged (by a faithful keeper of
    our hope, who came early) in careful rows on the cracked, scuffed,
    peeling linoleum floor,
we listen to tributes both flowery and plain, both fluent and stammering
(from the simple person who looks anxiously at the hero while speaking
and from the confident, experienced operative who, having lived far more
    than could be told, tells some of what remains to be lived),
and in the first row of chairs the hero bows her gray-haired head,
and the hour is passing,
and, because the old window that someone opened in order to let out
    the accumulated heat is letting too much cold from the brute night
    into the large shabby upstairs room, a woman from the back row of
    the folding chairs now disarranged on the cracked, scuffed, peeling
    linoleum floor goes to that window, and as quietly as she can, while
    another tribute is being offered, she draws it downward and closed
(although one pane is already broken out anyway
as if the hero herself, stronger than the rest of us, insisting
on our behalf, had arrived secretly before any of us and deliberately
    shattered it).

FIVE PEARS OR PEACHES

Buckled into the cramped back seat, she sings to herself as I drive toward her school through the town streets. Straining upward to see out her window, she watches the things that go by, the ones she sees—I know only that some of them are the houses we sometimes say we wish were ours. But today as we pass them we only think it; or I do, while she's singing—the big yellow one with a roofed portico for cars never there, the pink stucco one with red shutters that's her favorite. Most of what she sings rhymes as it unwinds in the direction she goes with it. Half the way to school she sings, and then she stops, the song becomes a secret she'd rather keep to herself, the underground sweetwater stream through the tiny continent of her, on which her high oboe voice floats through forests softly, the calling of a hidden pensive bird—this is the way I strain my grasp to imagine what it's like for her to be thinking of things, to herself, to be feeling her happiness or fear.

After I leave her inside the school, which was converted from an old house in whose kitchen you can almost still smell the fruit being cooked down for canning, she waves goodbye from a window, and I can make her cover her mouth with one hand and laugh and roll her eyes at a small classmate if I cavort a little down the walk.

In some of her paintings, the sun's red and has teeth, but the houses are cheerful, and fat flying birds with almost human faces and long noses for beaks sail downward toward the earth, where her giant bright flowers overshadow like trees the people she draws.

At the end of the day, her naked delight in the bath is delight in a lake of still pleasures, a straight unhurried sailing in a good breeze, and a luxurious trust that there will always be this calm warm weather, and someone's hand to steer and steady the skiff of her. Ashore, orchards are blooming.

Before I get into bed with her mother at night, in our house, I look in on her and watch her sleeping hands come near her face to sweep away what's bothering her dreaming eyes. I ease my hand under her back and lift her from the edge of the bed to the center. I can almost catch the whole span of her shoulders in one hand—five pears or peaches, it might be, dreaming in a delicate basket—till they tip with their own live weight and slip from my grasp.

ODE: CITIZENS

In the long shadows of the Chicago mountains, I walk past a very old
    woman, she's tiny, pushing down the sidewalk in the other direction a
    grocery-store basket overfilled with her homeless possessions without
    price, maybe she's

She's the same age as Mother, at the very end, she looks very like Mother,
    with the same large, startling, intense and made-up eyes, and she
    stares

And stares at me with autumn clarity, and when I look back at her she is
    still staring, having stopped and half-turned, but I go on—instead of
    responding to her and asking, "Auntie?"

And asking who she is, asking whom she recognizes in me, taking that
    opportunity of a split second to speak to this stranger, but it passes
    before I have let myself feel

Fully the impulse to speak, the need to speak, I move on, the distance

The gap between us is too great and I don't want to turn around and see if
    she is still watching me,

Maybe she is, I feel guilty—her existence is knowable but willfully not
    known by people like me—yet this is not an aunt of whom I never
    knew, nor is it Mother herself as I never knew her,

As I needed to know her, or rather as I needed her to be,

To be knowable to me emotionally,

To be capable of knowing me,

This is an old woman I don't know who could use twenty dollars and a
    different life,

A different history

For herself and for everyone,

And for her realness I await no metaphor (they do come when the arteries
of thought are calmly open),

This is not a moment amazingly full of a conversation that has never before
been spoken, a discovery to overturn everything, finally an exchange
of revelations.

|||||||

From somewhere, a family, a village, a neighborhood, comes

The solitary singer, maybe with a guitar, who pauses with her burdens and
sings, or the wayfaring man with a story that began somewhere else
who stops under a tree and plays a dance on his violin, even if no one
listens or dances,

Dances or even listens, for there is pain and there is hope—some of the
pain

Produced impersonally by remote traders in policy, some of the pain
produced

By an ever tighter knotting of constraints around our inward leap to escape,
some of the hope

Used against those who hope, postponing their desires and displacing
their attempts to choose onto clothes and stars and which streets to
wander.

|||||||

After a waitress brings three plates of hot food from which steam is rising
delicately, a thin woman in a booth behind mine in a diner says to
her two companions, "I only eat dark meat," her voice is apologetic,
she wants to be helped— "Actually, I only eat the wings . . . ," she
says,

"Really, I only eat part of the wings," she's about fifty, and the two men
     sitting opposite her, each with a glass of beer to wash down the grub,
     are in their seventies, and in a softer voice she says to the shorter one,
     "Can I call you Uncle Sid?"

And there seems to be a small party in the back room for a new young
     fireman, who will try to save the uncles who have built the diners and
     taverns and the aunts who have waited on the customers, and the
     customers, too, if they are caught inside the fiercest heat of what is
     burning us.

                              ||||||

Near me in a coffee shop are two imperfect persons in their forties, perhaps
     from the nearby halfway house, the woman is nodding, almost
     entirely silent, as the man talks and talks in halfway words, a kind of
     disabled philosopher giving a disjointed discourse

On beauty, on his fingers, on gaining exactly one pound of body weight last
     week, on Israel, but as if the woman weren't there,

Does she even know him?—and she nods to him with her upper body in
     a kind of self-restrained homage of rocking, he's her lost brother, she
     hopes or fears,

Neither of them has any longer the habit of combing or brushing hair, he
     half-rises, he leans across the table and kisses her cheek.

                              ||||||

Because in some village there will yet be a wedding that lasts three days,

Because sometimes the solitary singer, maybe with a guitar, pauses in
     her journey and sings, or the wayfaring man who knows a world
     somewhere else stops under a tree and plays a melancholy dance on
     his violin,

And after picking or threshing all day in Kosovo or Michoacán or
    Mississippi, singing softly together while riding in a tractor-cart, the
    harvesters go back tired to the small town to get a beer,

And in Illinois on the raw graded earth that will be a road the builders walk
    away from the monstrous machines turned off and turn on their own
    pickups, their radios shout,

And the late-night workers in Chicago restock the shelves or suit up in
    their clown costumes and begin to fry and sell hamburgers or in their
    pajamas they strain motionlessly over the report that is due, because
    there is resignation yet there can still be a plan.

IIIIIII

The city's restless movement never ceases in the streets, everyone has things
    to do, and on the same streets the beggars and wanderers and the
    out-of-work and the thinkers and the grieving do almost nothing,
    and in offices people are performing or pretending or laughing at a
    whispered joke, they are laboring against a deadline or wasting the
    clock, and after a manager has surveilled the cubicles and returned to
    his office, their hands are still holding pens that must ultimately leave
    marks of anger and desire and calculation.

IIIIIII

In a class I was teaching at a literacy center, I was talking about some
    sentences, some lines of a poem, some feelings, and interrupting me
    a tired woman of about thirty-five began to speak to me urgently, I
    listened, her face showed the intensity of a struggle within herself,

But what could she do, and how could I help her, she said, if from as early
    as she could remember, for her whole life, nobody had told her
    nothing?

Nothing. Her strong, somehow crooked face, her chipped tooth. Her
    solitary path to this moment—we all understood that she had come
    all this way without mother or father.

And an older woman sitting next to her put an arm around her after she
   had asked the unanswerable questions and together they cried softly.

Softly I said the word that I had learned was her scarred name,

Betty, I said, What you have just asked us all, this is what you know, this is
   what you have in yourself to tell us, to give to us, that we need.

AVIAN TIME

The collection manager of the bird specimens at the natural history museum told of often stopping, on his way to work during spring and fall, at the immense convention building—tall, long and wide—on the shore of Lake Michigan, where on the north side he would gather the bodies of the migratory birds killed by their collisions against the expanse of glass before first light.

The north side, whether in fall or in spring—a puzzle.

Are these particular birds blown off course by winds, and do they return in starlight or dimness before dawn or under dark clouds toward shore, making for the large bulk they might perceive as forest?

They have been flying along this same route for tens of thousands of years, and not yet has their thinking formulated this obstacle of the city that has appeared in the swift stroke of a hundred and fifty cycles of their migration.

ELSEWHERE CHILDREN

In the icy block between Madison and Monroe,
walking slowly and unbalanced
by the two unequal bags of layers of
bags of apparently nothing,

she who was once somebody's darling—
and the somebody lost to her, years
ago, and forgotten, maybe, along with birthdays
and beatings and other things that were best

forgotten—has stopped in a doorway.
Two persons come walking by her unaware,
a young woman who is saying, "There's *something*
I need, not sure what," and a young man

with goatee and thin dirty gloves
who answers, "You looking for a man to protect you!"
This woman he's been wishing for and has
just met frowns and slows down;

with her "I'm all right" they stop near
the old one's shallow niche out of the wind.
(What cold hand turned her this way? When?
Last year? Or the year she was four

or five, so long ago?) The young woman
stamps her cheap sleek boots in the salty slush
and splashes the man's wet running shoes,
she says, "I'm hungry," and he answers, hoping

maybe coffee will be enough for her, "My son says
Daddy you going to eat eggs this morning?—
I say no more, man, not no more! I heard they
really bad for you!" And he laughs down at the shoes

so useless to him, at the wonder of a world
beyond his powers. The old woman squints up at him
but the young one with him only says,
looking off, "My little girl's seven."

Separate parents, she and he, of elsewhere children.
(Where did the old woman's father leave her
one day, the start of the path here,
if just with a way of saying no or yes?)

My own dearborn, away from me today,
with secrets already of puzzling
not quite thinkable harm
(I know, because at my slight warnings

sometimes inside you a troubling echo
I can't hear alarms you, you say
"Don't tell me that or I'll worry
about it all night and I won't be able to sleep!")—

my only-five-years-old, with a soul
already taught by pain to be articulate
and beginning already to wrinkle, let no day
or disappointment ever turn you

toward a street as cold and hungry as this.
Let someone show me please how to keep
you from it if I can, if they can.
As for wishing you always free of ordinary pain,

like a father's or a mother's, I might
as well wish food into dead refrigerators
and the warmth to come out of these store windows
into the street and do some good.

Then the young woman and man walk away.
And she who was once somebody's darling
blinks them away and gone in the between-buildings light,
they could be her children, she was once

someone's, but she can't look after them,
we can't look after our own.

A CAR

It was past midnight when Andrea, exhausted but still not able to sleep, put aside the book she was trying to read in bed because she heard loud men's voices, two of them, out in the street, all the louder for the quietness of the snow-covered night along her city block of close-set brick two-flats. Then the wheels of a car spinning, the engine racing, whining—someone stuck. But there was an ominous sound to it; it didn't seem like neighbors. The men were yelling at each other but with a laughter that sounded giddy and somehow dangerous. Maybe stoned or drunk.

She sat up slowly, cautiously, as if they might hear her and know that somebody, she in particular, was listening, was aware of them, and they would not want her to know they were out there. Willie sat up at the foot of the bed, having ridden her legs like a cat as she moved them under the covers. He was staring at her, not barking at the noise outside. She threw back the covers and swung her legs over the edge of the bed and stood up quietly, quietly. And took one step, then another, then a third, and she was at her cold window. She moved as deliberately as a street mime to put her eye at the narrow vertical gap between the window shade and the frame.

There was no one in sight; but a long, dark car, kind of old, was parked haphazardly, at a slight angle, across the street, not any of the neighbors' cars. Maybe that was a movement, somebody hastening, just going around the far corner, which she noticed too late, for whoever it was, was gone. Willie was standing at her ankles, interested in what Andrea might do. He yapped once, looking up at her, eager.

She went back to bed—less cautiously than she had gotten out of it—and pulled the covers over herself. Willie leapt up with an effort and settled himself again on her legs. Before she slept, Andrea tried for another hour to read her book, a novel about England in the 1920s; she slipped in and out of it as other thoughts raced sometimes. There wasn't a sound from the Thompsons downstairs; they probably hadn't even heard anything, much less waked up.

In the morning she took Willie out at seven and dragged him through the snow to the alien car. It had Ohio plates, and a beat-up man's bull-rider western hat of straw lay precisely at the center of the rear deck. Over the back seat lay an old bedspread, and the car was pretty shot.

Willie hated to go out on the cold days—he didn't have enough hair to keep him anywhere near warm, and even though she put his little doggie sweater on him, he would stand shivering on the roofed porch and she had to drag him down the cement steps and along the sidewalk till he resigned himself to it and walked properly and did his business. Since he was as small as a cat, pulling him wasn't any trouble for Andrea, but she didn't feel good about it: he was helpless against her great power. However, he couldn't or maybe didn't reproach her.

With Willie in reluctant tow and seeming disoriented by her breaking of their routine, she walked around the car one time—more snow had fallen during the windy night, and there were no footprints she could see that would tell her for certain that this was the car she had heard. But she knew it was. A huge old Buick, dark green and dirty. She'd never seen it before. Stolen? She noticed it had a flat front tire on the passenger side; she figured that when the tire went flat they just gave up on it and walked away. Too stoned to care. They could steal another one—this one had gotten them all the way from Ohio.

On she went with Willie, around the block once, some of the sidewalk was shoveled already, some was not, she was thinking about the car, but looking at Willie she was also amused, as always, by his thinking he was a big dog.

The trains were running without delays, she opened the office, turned on all the lights, put the coffee on for everybody, changed the date on the wooden building-block office calendar, and gave Ramón—the next to arrive—the key to the P.O. box and sent him off into the snowy streets to get the morning's mail. The others staggered in, unwrapping their scarves and coats from their bodies, looking groggy and cold and out of sorts, and it took everybody till about ten, as usual, to say something pleasant to each other. Mr. Homburg had himself to blame, he was the one who set the sour tone of the place, but he blamed everyone else instead, all sixteen of them, for not being a happy office.

She ate lunch in the office kitchen, listening to the four adjusters play bridge, and reading every paragraph of the city section of the newspaper looking for anything suspicious. But of course the city was much too big, the newspaper was more for sports fans, celebrity lovers, political heads, and shoppers than anyone else, and nothing in her neighborhood would get reported unless it was a colossal crime or disaster.

When she got home at six in the dark, she noticed in the futile light from the street lamp that a fluorescent orange ABANDONED CAR sticker had been slapped onto the driver's side window. Usually, that took the city about six weeks to do, and it had only been one day. Somebody in the neighborhood must know something. Or somebody in the neighborhood who was especially annoyed had a relative on the force. She unlocked her foyer door, next to the Thompsons' door, locked it behind her and climbed the stairs; she had put a deadbolt on the upstairs door, too—after asking permission of the Thompsons. Inside, she put down her purse, kept her keys in her coat pocket, dressed the very excited but unwilling Willie in his sweater and hauled him down the stairs and into the cold. Alert and abstracted at the same time, she walked him around the block once more. The street was quiet, empty. She didn't see anyone else out; but the windows of most of the houses were lit and they looked pretty cozy inside. The city plow had come through and had had to swerve out and around the Buick, shoving a shin-high wall of snow and frozen slush up against it. Now Andrea saw from the walk in front of her own porch steps that somebody had started to scrape off the orange sticker with a knife or something but had stopped, and the Ohio plates were gone. Just in the ten minutes it had taken her to walk Willie around their block. But there was no one in sight.

Whoever had stolen it and brought it here was staying on the street somewhere, with someone. She picked Willie up and carried him into the foyer and let them both into her first door, and then for his last little bit of exercise she chased him cheerfully up the stairs with her to her second door.

Her apartment smelled stale. She switched on her radio to news and looked into her freezer for something to cook. Willie was trembling and yapping a little as he stood on his hind legs, pawing her calves. She pushed him away gently with one foot without even looking at him.

The inside of her refrigerator depressed her. She closed it and fed Willie and then went to her bedroom window in the front of the apartment and looked out at the car. Panting fast, Willie caught up with her after wolfing his food.

She resigned herself to cornflakes, and she let Willie lap the leftover sugar milk from the bowl. She turned off the radio. The better to listen to the sound, or rather quietness, of the night. The Thompsons' TV was on too loud, they were hard of hearing—good landlords to have on the first floor of the two-flat, too creaky themselves to climb up to her floor very often for a look. She got ready for bed early, and read till late; the TV sounds from below were still oozing through the floor when she fell asleep—movie music, loud voices.

The next morning she was a little late walking Willie, was afraid she would be late for work, and with her head down against the painful wind she hurried back into the foyer and was confronted by a strange man, about thirty-five, coming unshaven and mussed out the door of the Thompsons' flat. He was pulling their door shut behind him and he looked at her glancingly and went past her outside, wearing a thick sweater and over that a dark blue hooded sweat top that had a smear of white house paint on one sleeve. No coat. This had to be, Andrea felt it in the chilled hollow at the center of her chest, a man who had arrived in that car. He was in her building. What could he possibly have to do with the Thompsons?

Carrying Willie, she rushed upstairs and turned her deadbolt after them and stared for a moment at the pitifully thin wood of her door. Willie lay down in his little red-plaid bed, looking up at her. He barked at her once.

She pulled herself together and left for work, looking around her—the man was not in sight, the tire was still flat—as she walked to the station, as she stood on the windy cold platform, as she stood on the slow, swaying, jolting train all the way downtown and as she walked to her familiar building (which today seemed unfamiliar and strange as she noticed the age and dustiness of things she had never noticed before). She entered the silent empty office, which every day, before anyone else arrived, she alone had to fill with consciousness, with human presence. It had not occurred to anyone else how this exhausted her. And today even frightened her.

Lights, coffee, calendar, key for Ramón. And when he returned lugging the weight of paper in the plastic USPS bin, she had to remind him to give the key back to her, as she did almost every day, and he was never going to offer it until she asked. He seemed to like to resist, just slightly, doing what was expected of him by anyone, including Andrea; well, OK, if that's how he had to get through the day, then so be it.

There was something fateful about the Buick. It would affect her. She did not know how but was certain of that man crossing her life. Flung at her by his own ruthless stealing of the car. Did he know the Thompsons? Had he come to get something from them? Maybe it was he watching the TV late at night, not they.

There was no way to guard against something unexpected, invading, dangerous; this was life. Mr. Homburg sent for her, and when she was in his office he offered her two tickets to a Bulls game—her one turn had come for use of the company's pair of season tickets. She declined and excused herself without even making any small talk with him. He was still holding the tickets up in one hand and waiting to be thanked and flattered when she went out his door, past Alice at her desk positioned to guard his superiority—Alice putting on lipstick for the third or fourth out of her twenty or so times per day.

As Andrea came to the last block of her walk home from the station, she slowed her pace. Her heart thudded when she saw the stranger standing on the small front porch, smoking a cigarette, looking across the street at the skewed, abandoned, lifeless car. She had to go right up to him, past him. She kept walking toward him, she made herself think of Willie being amusing, she stared only at the front door as she went up the steps. Everyone had a story—except her, of course; she didn't think she could call her life so far any kind of story—and if she knew his, she thought, it would change something about what she thought, about how she felt. Well, that wasn't true in every case—she knew the stories of everybody at work. But she liked the idea. She believed in it, even if it wasn't true. He had the face of a thug. Or a pianist. Or an immigrant Marlboro Man. And what she had to do, she had to do for herself, not for him, not for the Thompsons. It all had to do with what or how she herself wanted to be, for her own sake.

MILWAUKEE & DIVISION

beginning with a line of Cyprian Norwid

If, instead of squinting out through windows
                    crusted with clear frozen gems, we
could freely watch glass monoliths float their
                    money heads through the sunny sky,
could see them strive up as they do when spring
                    veils them near the top in lengths of
cloud clinging like a gray-white scarf across
                    their throats; and if as spice to that
colossal dish we could see crabapple
                    and viburnum blossoms against
the preexisting cold cobalt-blue lake
                    and even catch the two heady
scents—one like delicate sweet ozone for
                    drying a wet soul, the second
a perfume for second-time brides . . . then an
                    avid desire to be awestruck
would best the foreboding on bitter streets,
                    the bored gaze at the sunset Oz-
ian or Ozymandian splendor
                    (before it's ruined by time and
climate yet to come) which to the east stands
                    spectacularly just as if
for a last curtain call. Things are other-
                    wise, though. On this street we hunger
for tacos, thirst for a beer, we regard
                    the triangular mazurka
of a square, the name of Chopin atop
                    a theater, a sky that wants to
make art, and through this door here, the wife who
                    carries to guests at her paying
kitchen tables her white borscht, stuffed cabbage,
                    potato-and-cheese pierogies,
and who's eaten in turn by an etching
                    we imagine, which contains her

and her diner, bad boys late at night, girls
                  also, good hopes and sad salsa
to season them, and rays of greedy light.
                  It's cold. Let's go in here and eat.

SMALL BUSINESS

Into the ground-floor, storefront office, past the three staff—the secretary ("Hello, boys, he's in his office"), the accountant (who is always annoyed at anything like this), and the assistant manager (who doesn't even notice them)—to the manager, come the two twelve-year-old boys.

The manager is rumpled, bent over his desk, scribbling something on a legal pad.

"Hi Dad, can you give us some money to go to McDonald's?"

"Hey." (Without looking up from his desk.) "Two hungry young men at large, alert all kitchens."

Then the manager stops writing, looks up and adds, "Why?—don't you have any money?"

"No—we want to go to McDonald's."

"It's four o'clock, you're going to be late for your game. Did you take the bus here?"

"No, we're not."

"Don't you have to be there by five?"

"It's not till five thirty."

"Oh. Did you take the bus?"

"So can we have some money?"

"Don't you have any left?"

"We were going to go to the bank, Jimmie was going to get some out of the bank, but it was closed."

"Jimmie—you have a bank account?" (The manager is surprised, curious.)

"Yeah. A savings account." (He is, in fact, holding a little blue book.)

"Oh." (To his son:) "Am I picking you up at home? You have to get your game stuff, right?"

"Yeah. But McDonald's?"

"You have money at home, right? I'm only loaning. How much have you got at home? When you go to McDonald's with friends, it's on your allowance, right?"

"At home I've got eight dollars."

"OK, here." (He counts out bills from his wallet.) "Take eight, and now you owe me your eight."

"Well—Mom owes me five, so you could just get that five from her, and I could give you three at home."

"She owes you five?"

"Yeah. Could you just give me ten? You have a ten?"

"What does she owe you five for?"

"Because she didn't have all my allowance on Saturday, and she still hasn't given it to me."

"That's not the way I remember it—I thought she was holding back five dollars for the comix you weren't supposed to buy."

"No—I don't have to pay her back for that, she said. Didn't she tell you?"

"No."

"She said that was OK because after I finish reading it again I'm going to give it to Brian. He's in the hospital with a broken leg. He broke it really bad."

"OK, but if you have eight dollars at home, you already owe them to me anyway, because remember I'm still waiting to get back the twenty dollars I gave you so you could pay for the jersey you lost at school, and you spent it on something else instead. This kind of thing—"

"That was on school supplies, remember? And you told me that was OK."

"—is important—to be responsible for your money, right?"

"You told me it was OK."

"I did? I don't remember that."

"Well, could we have ten dollars, Dad?"

"So if I give you ten, how much do you owe me?"

"Will I owe you something?"

"Yes, of course you will!—you'll owe me the ten bucks, I'm only loaning it to you, I said."

"Yeah, but that was before we talked about all the other stuff. You don't remember stuff, sometimes, Dad, like the twenty for school supplies."

"No, I think I would remember that."

"Please? You're going to get the ten dollars right back! Mom's going to give you five, and Jimmie's going to pay me back for his half."

"Look, just take the eight dollars and we'll talk about it when I get home. You have a little more time than I thought, but make sure you get yourself home and get your stuff together, and be ready to leave by ten after five, Mom and Dougie are picking me up, then I'm dropping them off at his peewee soccer practice, so I'm just stopping the car in front and honking the horn, and we're going straight there, OK? OK?"

"OK."

The boy grins winningly at his father, who smiles back at him with instantly helpless love and exasperation, and then he looks at the papers on his desk, to pick up what he had stopped working on.

Jimmie has not said a word. But he whispers to the manager's son as the two boys turn to go out, and the manager's son stops and asks, almost over his shoulder, "Are we going to get the car radio fixed?"

The manager does not look up from his pad. He says, "I don't know— get one for your bike."

"Yeah."

The two boys grin at each other and walk back past the assistant manager, the accountant, and the secretary. The manager calls after them, "Hey, how did you get here? Did you take the bus?" The secretary, sitting at a desk that is too small, is tapping a calculator and balancing her checkbook, which she is holding on her lap. The boys do not notice her, nor she them.

FORSAKEN IN THE CITY

What noise on the street rushing with cars and crowded with people under the apartments and church that tilt over sidewalks and shops, and inside a neighborhood corner grocer's store a loud radio and people choosing apples and cabbages and potatoes from stacked wooden crates and wicker baskets, what noise; and others inside have gathered butter and milk and cheese and loaves of bread in their arms, are crowding against the counter to pay, clamoring in two or three languages or silent, waiting. Outside on the corner, newspapers are stacked at the feet of a man who goes out into the street to hawk them when the traffic light turns red and the engine exhaust poisons the air. The heavy smell of frying wafts from the restaurants nearby. And past all the cars stopped or rolling slowly, inching forward, whose horns bleat up and down the echoing man-made canyons, here and there amid the roar is hidden the stillness before motion resumes and the stillness after motion has stopped, both stillnesses ceaselessly arriving and dissolving again into noise: in this person's sudden halting before a cold package of brats, a beautiful eggplant, in that one's closed eyes while standing at the bus stop. And the man on his way through, among all the others this one person whom we know so well, he is closer to us than a brother—he thinks he has just heard his name called out, quite clearly, he turns and looks back over his shoulder. He looks across the street, peers into the open doorway of the grocer and into a garage like a dry cave and into a dry cleaner, to find who it is amidst this din, if it is anyone, who knows him. The sound glittered like a gem discovered among pebbles in shallow clear water and it caught him abruptly and made him forget what he'd been thinking. But he doesn't hear his name called again, no one looks familiar, he must have heard it in some other name or call, some play of sound that his mind seized mistakenly from the noise to make the similar seem the identical. Did he hear it because without any awareness of his feelings he had wanted to be called, to be summoned? It was his childhood nickname, a name for all of his being that was hidden inside his adult life, not the name anyone now calls him by, it would be a misnaming in their mouths, and he looks here and there and sees no one he might know from back then, no one he recognizes. Maybe it's someone he can't recognize any longer. Above the street are faces in windows; in this one and that, someone is looking down. The late afternoon's hot and in that window or this comes a glimpse of someone inside who is moving across a darkened room. And above them are the roofs with no one on them at all except for one strange creature who might have wings and who seems disappointed; turning back from the edge, where she was standing only an instant before, looking down, her call still echoing, she is about to fly away.

A LARGE HEAVY-FACED WOMAN,
POCKED, UNKEMPT, IN A LOOSE DRESS

. . . and her mute shadow touching me
made me look up, the glass panes
and squatting aircraft like a movie screen
behind her, and she smiled, held out
a small orange card that I took
with my hand from her hand—

the deaf-and-dumb alphabet on one side,
hand-signs, and on the other her plea,
her exhortation, her prayer, her pitch:
SMILE. With the fingers that took my coins
she drew a blessing in the air and
like a tired usher walked away
down the empty seats and dirty ashtrays

to a young woman with a baby, the orange
card hovered till the child stirred,
reaching up, reaching, the mother lifted
her head from her worries to frown,
say no. Maybe someone was late.
Or hadn't caught the right plane or had
caught it, leaving; or left with bad words.

The big woman shaped another smile with her lips,
touched the baby's curling wafted hand,
traced her blessing again, wasted no words.
Her limp fingers invisible with the silence
of their stillness, down the narrowing corridor
she went toward the next gate, where some
gathered oblivious drunk traveling men

wearing cowboy hats and boots after their convention
were singing the loud song she couldn't hear
as she approached them like the stage messenger
whose surprising words will signal the end but

who says nothing this time, and the singing stops,
the actors stand in place waiting, and the audience,
restless and embarrassed, begin to bark into their hands

willing now to welcome any word, even the bad news
The Queen is dead, or The old shepherd
whom you summoned knows, or I alone escaped to tell thee.
But she doesn't speak, only her hands can—like yours,
you accoutered conventioneers and you grievers,
you tired mothers, you healers and whores on trips,
wife-beaters and tormentors of children,

you shoe-salesmen, cooks, polite cold freeway toll-takers
with warm palms, you men making fists
in your compulsive pockets around coins or keys,
you women groping in purses for cigarettes,
for candy and gum and lipstick confused,
here is your herald! Some message is come.
Even the worst she can say will be touching.

And your being still could be a kind of listening.

ADMIRATION

The autumn day dark early

Windy rain approaching from the prairie

like a stranger from the prairie

And down between great buildings on the shadowed city street someone
sheltered in the cold chapel of an unused doorway
with another blind paper cup at his feet
was playing on a saxophone
he had brought with him in a shopping bag
the classics of improvisation

                    the great tunes
the riffs of his tradition
               the changes

handed down again just now by him

And in the pushing wind, the certainty of rain, soon—
who stopped for a moment to listen and pitched
his own voice to the blue note
and a few coins into the cup?

A LEAP

Gallery 109, by Tadao Ando (1992), The Art Institute of Chicago

Not always but
sometimes, sometimes—
I, unmoving,
they, unmoving—
I watch for a
while the sixteen
squared columns of
wood—smooth, polished,
dark, in a dark
room—standing all
together, and
I imagine
others—of type,
of marble, of
red granite, that
like these refuse
to hold any-
thing up—nothing
atop them (no
capitals, no
architraves, no
pediments, no
rafters, no roofs;
no temples, no
courts, no markets,
no banks, spires, or
legislatures,
no slaves, no lost
cause, crops, cannons,
accords, foreign
debts, recessions,
no mandates, no
systems, newscasts,
or calendars):

I begin at
their feet and move
my gaze upward
along them, then
at the tops I
feel the next look
as a leap of
my body off
free columns toward
anything or
anyone freed.

MEKONG RESTAURANT

What is the half-life of a city?

There are green shoots of rice, a soft diaphanous green undulating, shimmering, in a breeze over the flat surface of water, outside a village of tiny frail huts with talk in them, under trees of a rainy hot climate, washed in rain, in a country of rain clouds and war.

A menu in Vietnamese and English.

A dozen immigrants waiting among native and naturalized citizens for their boxes and bags inside a terminal at O'Hare. Refugees have streamed back the way that war came to them—into the very country that had turned the fire on them. With them they've brought their children and their names. Some of their children; some of their parents; names that must struggle to be pronounced inside unfamiliar mouths.

But these streets blow with a wind of ice. Or in summer they show a jewel-glitter sparkling like sequins on fields of green and gray—innumerable bits of shattered glass on raw vacant lots between crumbling apartment blocks and ramshackle three-flats. Up and down the busy street there are shops, Viet Hoa Market, Nha Trang Restaurant, Video King, White Hen, Viet Mien Restaurant, McDonald's, Dr. Ngo Phung Dentist, Nguyen Quang Attorney at Law, Viet My Department Store. High and far as mountains beyond and above the two-story roofs of this street, the winter gray-on-white cityscape wears banners of steam flapping straight sideways in the bitter wind. If you stare at the big buildings long enough you might begin to sense a fundamental instability in the balanced masses and you might wonder why they don't just fall.

Go out into a park field and hide under a weed.

Same moon, not the same moon. After danger and escapes, after feeling so intensely the desire to live, to live in such a place will make some feel they have come to their own funeral. To live away from your own place, to live far away from your own place, and to think you will never return, is to be condemned to have been saved one time too many, some will feel.

When meteor showers fall next summer, you won't see them because the underbelly of the sky is lit orange all night in every season. But the children are growing accustomed. This is where their friends are.

An immigrant boy of fourteen wearing black trousers and a white shirt and a thin jacket is standing with his immigrant parents at the counter of the high school office, waiting to be called in to be registered; the clerks are busy, paying the immigrants no mind, and the mother and father and boy are waiting. At this school the students speak twenty-nine native tongues, or forty-four, or sixty-seven.

One hears stories of the city. Some legendary summer evening of decades ago, across the deep street chasms from the important, wealthy, powerful white men served by black men in a private twenty-fifth-floor men's club, among the columns of the little Greek rotunda atop the twentieth-something-floor roof on the other side of Michigan Avenue, hired for this occasion, some white women wearing only very diaphanous gowns, specially floodlit, shimmering, unreachable, danced while the club members ate their evening meal. Most of the money is in some people's hearts; most of the fear is in other people's pockets.

The year lasts longer here. This is a proven fact of quantum physiology: that time passes more slowly when the air is cold than when it is warm; and that ice is radioactive when it touches the human body; and that hyperdiodes of mortal irradium glow before they shatter into ice.

Nearby are two zoos, many banks, millions of persons, and the inland sea, frozen for a long way out, and hills of ice that have risen along the beaches, and blackened piles and heaps of decayed snow beside the lakefront roads where the traffic is always speeding by.

A menu in English and Vietnamese.

It's late, the immigrant boy is looking out, from beside the honest stove, through the kitchen pickup window, at the way it is now, at three American strangers, still in their overcoats, who have come in, who are looking around, who are sitting down hesitantly at a table.

It's a Saturday. What is the half-life of a city?

CITY

Again in this early spring
the scents of wet earth and
new green arrive
like hesitant recruits in the old
neighborhoods. The handsome
and ugly brick buildings
whisper their forgotten war
stories to the acidic city
air night and day,
in snow and sun, presiding
over streets named for
forgotten local Shermans
and Grants who used to gather
with their admirers in the old
forerunners of these present-
day eateries and bars—
the insider reticence, the cool
iced tea and beer in summer,
shots and hot coffee
in winter, among the ex-
officers and enlisted men,
soldiers and sailors who did
something for the Union . . .

Then came the Great Fire,
then the double-zero year,
then another war, and electricity—
safer than gas—and automobiles
got heavier and faster,
the horses gone, the veterans
of the Great War came home

looking for work, worked,
some of them kept tiny
gardens on their back landings
and in window boxes . . .

Clean-shaven, short-
haired young men
in jackets and ties who had
graduated or not from
the old high school
made lives or lost them
on the job or in the big
next war, the next
and the next. Finally the settlement
house that had seen off
a whole long-ago regiment
closed, the Wobblies' hall
became a rock club,
the grocery store small offices,
the theater a maze of video
rentals, comics, pillows,
candy and jeans and shoes,
the church is vacant, someone
removed the small memorial
tablet that remembered eighty
or one hundred bronze
names from this unpolished parish.

On a Saturday morning in
the old hardware store
with scuffed wooden floors,
an old man helps me—
so present to me that he
fully commits me
to his cause—which is only
that he knows of or will
discover everything that might
be asked for in such
a store: a man's kind
knowledge. He finds
exactly the few oddments
I am seeking and then
with a miniature key in his hand

he goes to a glass cabinet,
he unlocks it and reaches in
to get for me the small
knife I want to buy.

My little daughter was with me
that day, he smiled at her
and asked her where she
was going to school and when
she told him, he said
that was where he'd gone,
too, when he was a boy.
"That one, and then the middle
school, *and* the high school, too.
But I wasn't smart—I left
the high school before
I graduated," he was saying.
"Went into the army.
Funny thing is,
my son did exactly the same
in World War Two."
He handed me the knife.
"I had three sons
in World War Two."
He returned the key to his pocket.
"Two of them didn't come back."
Without making any
sound he started to cry
and turned half away
to half touch at his eyes
with his thick fingertips. "It killed
my wife. Took nine years
to do it, but it killed her."
He looked at us again.
Recovering.

　　Shying. "Anything
else you need?" He touched

my child's hair for an instant.
"I grow tulips. Have
a thousand of them now.
My whole back yard's
tulips, the front yard, too.
The best ones are from
Holland, you know."
                    How
often does the defining
pain still come
through him?
                    He bent down
toward the small girl,
my child, and said to her,
"You'd like seeing them. They're
pretty little fellows."

WONDER

Along the dark neighborhood sidewalk, waddling toward the moonlit limitless lake six blocks away, a casual and brazen raccoon seems to expect me to stand out of its way. I certainly do. The sudden chill of adrenaline has put my skin and limbs on alert. Other improbable sightings of the other residents of this coastal plain have marked the problematic passage of recent human seasons—a running, frightened, confused deer clattering its small hooves down our own street of silent houses early on a Sunday morning, far from any woods; a red fox that trotted out of a patch of hedge and across my path as I was walking from one building to another; in a tall bush, the rare warbler lit by a shaft of sunlight on a windy, cloudy morning at Montrose Point; and one bright afternoon when inside the house I heard faraway continuous honking of Canada geese, finally I went outside to see how there could be so many. I looked up through the sunlit limitless spring sky at endless interconnected irregular skeins of them all, so far up, flying southwest, V and V and V and V branching again and again from each other, thousands and thousands of geese, honking en masse to make their continuous goose music, and entirely, amazingly, across the whole sky, the sky from church roof to treetops and house chimneys. Goose music was filling even the neighborhood's hot dusty attics, alleyway garages, basements. Fifty thousand geese, a hundred thousand, how many? In the small gravel parking lot of the small brick church, three or four neighbors and I stood with heads back, not speaking, watching the geese wavily pattern the whole sky the way waves pattern the lake, till after twenty minutes of watching, that immense, inconceivable effort of birds was more than our minds could reach toward any more; it dwarfed our imaginations, it exhausted our attention, it tired our feeble necks, it was like a mythical visitation on which human beings were perhaps not even to look. Yet for their ordinary every-year reasons they were crossing the sky that they filled with wing beats. We understood we would not be able to see the whole great expanse of them, they would never stop, they would beat their way through the exalted air over the vast city forever, the sky had become a place that always has geese in it.

ODE: AT A TWENTY-FOUR-HOUR GAS STATION

At a twenty-four-hour gas station and garage and dingy Food Mart on a
 city corner of unending traffic, next door to a chain restaurant that
 serves breakfast and inert heavy pie all day and night,

Around cold midnight, around the front end of my car with its hood up,
 five young guys from Mexico, not like me, their fathers could be on
 farms, are crowding in, staring at the workings, and the knowing
 one, after an hour and a half of waiting for the replacement parts to
 be delivered and after having worked on other cars in the meantime,
 teaching the others,

Is replacing the busted radiator, more for his audience than for me, and I
 remember seeing

Seeing in Mexico, not like here, a market where beside each stall of alert
 flowers on display for those who walked by, and beside each pyramid
 of wakeful mangos, papayas, tomatoes, bananas, oranges, peppers, sat
 the one who sold them, a human representative of both bounty and
 deprivation, of commerce and labor, waiting,

But here the one who sells his labor must not wait,

And waiting, I in my turn have come out to see what's happening, I've gone
 back inside, I've pissed in the grimy men's room, I've come out again,
 I've gone back over my resolutions and regrets, out of nowhere I've
 felt that familiar pang of longing for someone loved who is elsewhere,
 I'm checking my watch,

The other guys are watching, joking, not wearing enough clothes against
 this chilling world, and unpaid, they're learning,

I'm learning how knowledge is passed on so that more young men can
 make some money with their hands,

You can make money with your hands, your speed, your back or your
     brain, and with what's between the truth and a lie, what's between
     your legs, you can make money,

Money was not the first thing on my mind long ago

When I was young, for me learning was something in books, books were
     not inert but sometimes would seem about to beat like wings in my
     hands, I wanted all the books I could get and I thought that enough
     money would somehow come,

It comes in steadily here to the two owners, partners, Italian, not like me,
     they preside in shifts over the garage, the half-empty store, the cooked
     coffee, "Free" says the sign, in a dusty half-empty carafe on a hot hot
     plate, over the grimy restrooms and the space beside them, a kind of
     waiting room—

Three waiting beat-up conjoined seats transplanted from some failed
     theater.

||||||

I go inside and sit down for a while longer in an end seat, and in the other
     one now, one empty seat between us, is an old man, not like me, I
     saw him earlier talking with the night-owning Italian, he's resting
     both his big hands on a hand-carved cane with a wooden handle
     shaped like a dull axe blade, he's wearing a Greek sailor cap at a
     jaunty or negligent slant,

You dress good, he says to me, but I'm wearing nothing special, and because
     so often I feel on guard against others, that's the way I learned to be, I
     had deliberately not greeted him with my eyes as he watched me,

Now his accent tells me he's from here, because

Here is a place of eighty different accents, a city neighborhood of ugly and
     not expensive two-flats and four-flats and frame houses, houses of
     plans for the future and of families finished and dispersed, of old

worlds that don't fit, of children who love their grandparents and are ashamed of them, of short sprees and long hard hours, of dwellings corroded by the blowing urban exhalations,

Breathing hard, here some men and women have escaped a mortality elsewhere—Little Rock or Sarajevo—or have fallen across oceans from Saigon or Beirut into a mortality here, the storefronts speak

In tongues, the air is thick with speech, with grime, mistaken beliefs, odors of commercial cooking, gasoline, this is city air, and

And the old man, a city creature, wants conversation and

And to save my mortal soul for a few minutes, I turn to him and yield my gaze,

Guess, he says, where I'm from, You'll never guess.

IIIIIII

I guess Poland and he's startled but also pleased that he has not stumped me,

He stamps the cane and tells me his story

(Part of it: Jewish, he survived, he doesn't tell me how, he stayed in Warsaw till the 1950s, a tailor, he came to this country, to Chicago—Like coming through door, he says, I think I understand what he means— and he worked for years in clothing, he brought this cane all the way with him, he takes it wherever he goes, nowadays he has a big stall in a weekend flea market, keeps everything stored out there during the week, has good quality clothes, Come see, he lives two blocks from here, every evening he leaves his wife, she doesn't go out anymore, he comes over here to the garage, he sits for an hour or two and drinks the bad free coffee, even late at night he talks with anyone who might sit down near him to wait),

This place is all there is in this part of the world for him to use

The way he once used cafés in Warsaw

(In Warsaw, before his escape from those systems of bureaucracies of fear,
     he could not have foreseen this system's negligence and its clamoring
     transmitted voices and fantastic products and incrustations of fantasy
     but he hoped for livelihood and found it),

Cardin, Claiborne, Calvin Klein, Tommy, he says proudly, You save money,
     Is biggest flea market, Hundreds vendors, Ev'ryt'ing, Come see good
     clothes on weekend, You coming?

I tell him one part of my story: not from Warsaw but from Łodz and before
     that, Bialystok, came my maternal Jewish grandparents, a hundred
     years ago, I was right, he says proudly, I say you look like man from
     Europe,

So I say, Half of me,

And I see my father's young ghost running away again from the Mississippi
     farm of his Irish father and half-Choctaw mother and I see his old
     ghost backing away from this conversation and I ask the old man,
     What's your name?

||||||

Bill, he says, he smiles, and a disheveled, easy-gaited man of thirty or
     so, not like me or Bill, carrying an already disordered section of a
     newspaper, comes past us and without trying the doorknob of the
     men's room he goes straight into the ladies'—Bill and I hear distinctly
     the click of the lock

And we look at each other, I'll be back, I say, and I go out to the garage and
     the fifth young man is still working on the radiator, explaining to
     the other four what he's doing, they all smile at me, they're shivering
     and laughing and talking shit at each other, again I think of or am
     thought of by someone far away whom I miss and want to see again,
     right now,

When Bill sees me coming back he tilts his head toward the ladies' room
and raises his eyebrows to tell me the guy is still in there, and as soon
as I sit down again a young woman comes past us, her face showing
her distress, not like mine,

She's dressed inexpensively but very nicely, with smart shoes, I see that
Bill has appraised her clothes, anyone would say she has a beautiful
mouth, she comes past us and then the locked doorknob of the ladies'
stops her, she glances at us in embarrassment, in need, The men's is
empty, I say politely to her, and she looks offended that I have spoken
to her at all and she retreats out of sight

And Bill sighs, shrugs his shoulders at me, says, Do you believe?

Men once believed in gods, I say,

That's true, he answers, But anything can be doorway, if you give it push:
working with hands—you see these hands?—or philosophy; or seeing
people around you suffer; or piece of epple pie; or live with your own
t'oughts, day after day where you don't see no one else has t'oughts
like that; or even clothes . . .

Or a woman's beautiful mouth? or five young men talking in Spanish
around a radiator at midnight? I ask,

And Bill says, Yes, of course! Or cane!—and he raises this dark worn
wooden object so that I will see that on the handle, the head, are a
dozen little jangling tarnished rings on tiny posts, the cane seems
almost capable of knowing, of seeing, or even speaking,

Then we hear the toilet flushing and the guy comes out, no longer carrying
the newspaper, and he saunters away,

The bad dust on everything is like powdered herbs of neglect and death-
money,

I can smell the cheap thick cooked coffee,

The young woman returns rushing into the ladies', the faithful door offers
the guarantee of its locking click, library-ships that were intended to
arrive at faraway places of no books are sinking, the mass media are
a junkyard of new cars, and the miners are lying sick in their shacks,
money comes first, everything is the same as always and always
changed, lilies or papayas or midnight repairs, blue jeans or stories,
and in this moment as in every moment there is some possibility that
the last moment did not have, some other jalapeño or orchid or high
heel, some other radiator repair, some other young man who has left
home to find work,

And Bill is looking at me, and every messianic, apocalyptic or ordinary
hour of night and day, like this hour, seems infinite,

I ask him, Why are you here so late tonight, Bill? Don't you usually go
home by now?

The Italian on duty hastens across the cement Food Mart floor into the
garage, loudly calling one of his workers, Bill and I watch him,
Chicago is not like Italy or Mexico or Poland but Poland, Mexico,
and Italy are here in the garage, I know and I don't understand this,

Bill holds out his wrinkled heavy hand

To shake my hand, to offer and to receive honor and acknowledgment, we
have mortal souls

And our souls need continual repair,

Don't know why, Bill says—Workings of whole earth, I t'ink about, they
keep me up in middle of night—clothes, bills, what newspapers say,
then if I sleep I have bad dream, no, is good to sit here longer, talk,
till you go. Then I go.

ENOUGH

> Walking in a small park,
I ask myself what to
> think of Thebes, Leeds, Baghdad,
Dacca, Lagos, Lhasa,
> Rome, Prague, Perth, La Paz, Guam,
Ho Chi Minh, Pskov, Łodz, Durg,
> Dresden, Elabuga.

IIIIIII

Constant splashing of the
> fountain—shapeless water
thrown from beaks of iron birds,
> tall cranes, into the all
ways yielding air, air strong
> enough, though, to carry
on its bright back the scents
> of yellow, red, peach, pink
petals on this cloudy
> morning of cool summer,
the white light is wrong, it
> is sifting down as slow
as snow, church bells, nine times,
> make a dull comforting
sound but cannot make sense.

IIIIIII

Alone till now, I hear
> others nearby, and led
into this flower park
> by her grandmother comes
on tiptoe a pale small
> girl with straight red hair, in
a fine blue dress and white
> stockings and shiny shoes,

they're red, too, abruptly
         she pulls her hand free, with
her own flourishing she
         prances ahead on the
as yet untrodden, art-
         fully raked gravel walk,
she's enough for herself.

|||||||

I yield to her her place,
         retreat to a bench that
says who it remembers,
         as I'm always doing,
the little girl laughs with
         joy at the cranes, joy's real,
the water and cranes real,
         among these quiet streets,
in the midst of lucky
         houses never damaged.

THE VANISHING POINT

A young man with very bad teeth and a walleyed gaze, holding some poster boards on his lap, where they sagged on each side, and drawing on the top one with an old chewed ballpoint pen.

It was a severely rectilinear highway scene: a powerful exaggerated vanishing point puckering the empty horizon, lanes of cars coming on—as yet only outlined—and lanes of big trucks going away, already finished. One after another, all alike, semitrailers with company names on them, and all the perspective acutely correct. It all looked to have been drawn with a ruler, strictly and slowly; but he was doing it freehand, each stroke of the pen absolutely precise. Or rather, as imprecise as the human hand, but with an authority that could convey and even create precision in your eyes as you watched. Even the lettering he was putting on the side of the last, closest, largest trailer was as if painted by machine, and he never paused to consider proportions or angles, but simply kept drawing and darkening the shapes with the blue ink, as if he were tracing with quick uncanny dash a faint design already there on the white floppy board.

This was at Chicago and State, in the subway station.

A woman happened to come stand near him, and watched as he worked with his intent rhythm, his head bobbing and sometimes with his face low to study his work closely with one eye at a time. She watched, and he noticed her and smiled a wrecked-tooth wide blind-man's smile at her, and said, more than asked, "Nice work, idn't it!" She put her right thumb up and smiled back at him, and said nothing, and he lifted the top board and showed her the finished one underneath, for an instant—another roadscape, in colors, filled in and alive, the whole huge white board crammed with convincing and convinced detail.

"Nice work, idn't it!" he said again, and showed her the one underneath that one. Again, thumb up, and she too smiled happily—a wholly natural acknowledgment of him, an unsurprised understanding of his talent. She didn't act as if it seemed strange to her that he was sitting on a worn drab bench on the subway platform, next to the tracks, working in the dim light while commuters and others stood around waiting impatiently for the next train. It didn't seem to strike her that he was crazy and half-blind. That his work was driven, obsessively scrupulous, uninhabited, repetitive, brilliant, rhythmical, depthless, spiritless, useless.

"Nice work, idn't it!" he said to her each time, and he showed her—and me, because I too was standing there—six or eight more drawings: the Sears Tower, the skyline along Michigan Avenue, traffic in the streets, not a single person. The long lines were perfectly straight but when you looked at them more carefully they zigged with freehand force across the board in spurts. And her thumb went up to each in turn, and she smiled and each time she did, he said, "Nice work, idn't it!"

"I do nice work!" he said. "I did *all* these, and not a *single mistake*! Nice work!" he was saying as the train came in like sandpaper, hissing and braking. She walked away toward it without saying goodbye, and he looked at me, then. "Nice work, idn't it!" he said, as cheerfully as a man could ever say it.

"It's beautiful!" I said. The doors of the train opened a few feet away and everyone was stepping inside. "It's nice *work*!" he said, smiling, and I moved to the train and stepped in, the great force in him holding me to him still, and with part of myself I wished that it would win, but I did get in, the last passenger, and the doors shut and immediately the train jerked and began to roll out of the station and away.

JUST IMAGINE

Long ago, if you had gone to the window where my first lipstick left a mouth on the glass that I wiped off with toilet paper, and you had looked out at as sharp an angle as you could get, your cheek to the cold glass that was so dirty on the outside, you could have seen that, just as anybody would think but Mama, there was nothing out there on the other side of the fifth-story wall of our living room except the wind that blew around the tall apartment buildings night and day. (To me they seemed tall.) I had kissed the cold window, like saying a prayer please let there be something more for us like she says. But I knew there couldn't be. Mama was convinced sometimes—I'm not sure it was all the time—that if only we could secretly break through the living-room wall, the same wall where the picture of her mother had hung for so long, then we would find another room that nobody knew about. That no one but us would be able to use. A room just for us—Mama, Donald, Desmond, Bobo, and me. "I'm telling you! Go look out the window on that side and you'll see it," she would say hoarsely to me sometimes. She said it like it would be my fault if I didn't see it waiting for us. And if I had seen it . . . we still couldn't get to it.

Mama almost never went out, so we had to get everything for her, when we got ourselves organized and the money was there. In the living room, the bedroom, and the kitchen, which was the whole apartment, there was also, most of the time, Aunt Jean, Mama's younger sister who talked very loud even though she wasn't hard of hearing, Zulie, who was loud, too, but since she wasn't around very much she had a lower average loudness, you could say. And Bobo, yapping. And when Donald was a baby it seemed like he cried about the same number of hours every day that working people worked. Desmond was always a quiet boy. Mama almost whispered instead of talking, so you had to get very close to her to hear her, which was what she wanted. And me. But I'm not criticizing them—knowing what I know now. I wish I could go back there now; I wish I could just come through a door from that imaginary room and say, I've got a big meal waiting for you! And see them all crowding in like Christmas.

The secret room had a deep green carpet. And a little piano. And a big lamp with a decorated shade that made a soft yellow light, and a big red easy chair just for reading. It had pictures on the wall. It had lots of windows, but the room was never cold. And the city looked different through them—lights in those office buildings and skyscraper apartments were kind of cheerful and cozy instead of far off and lonesome, they said come over this way for a while, even though I had never been over that way, never had been to where those mountain-buildings were. The secret room had a dark brown wooden bookcase with books in it. And it was quiet in there. Oh, you could still hear the talking and noise from the living room and bedroom and kitchen, but muffled by the shut door. You could have laid down on the clean carpet and stretched yourself out any way you wanted and slept, it was that clean. No Bobo piss. No dust and dirt. And nobody stepping on you when they went by. Nobody shouting.

Mama was smart, she was determined, and if she had had some opportunities, if she had gotten some schooling, she might have been president of a company instead of turning into a woman who was not completely in touch with reality. Especially after she had her kids, and never had a husband. I'd look in my head for something I could actually say to her, and then I'd say it, so she wouldn't think I was sulking. So I grew up quiet, like Desmond. He and I. But my not saying much could make Mama angrier. Poor Mama. Nothing ever went right for her.

The roofs of our building and the three others like ours were flat. The last staircase, above where the elevator stopped on the twelfth floor, went up very steep to a door that opened on the roof. No one was supposed to go there. That door was supposed to be locked but the lock was always being broken. For a while somebody tried a big chain and padlock on it, but people knew how to break that, too. The roof was black, dried tar or something, so if you walked on it the soles of your bare feet, in summer, or your shoes in cold weather, got covered in a black powder. Inside the twelfth-floor hallway there were always black tracks on the floor. And just like on the ground around the building, there was junk up there, too— bottles and cans, some old wood or metal things, busted up, lying here and there. There was a low wall around the edge. But something was beautiful about being up there in good weather. You had to be careful, though, not to go up there when the wrong people might be there, too, or might come up on you.

The clouds moved, the sun moved, and in the daytime, the lake changed deep blue to light blue, blue to gray, gray to silver. At night, it made this edge of complete black *nothing* beyond the big buildings, there wasn't one bit of light in it. Hard to describe that feeling—it was like everything, everything, ended at the edge of the lake and there wasn't anything else there—no water, no ground, not even any air, nothing. Except when the moon would lay down this pale rippling kind of path across it to us that once in a while from our roof you could see between the skyscrapers.

I would find the right spot up there and kneel down at the edge, holding onto that little wall, and look over, straight down the side of the building where our apartment was, and count the floors down to the fifth, and I could sort of see where Mama's secret room would be, sticking out from the side of the building, if it had been there.

I'd feel sorry for her and ashamed of myself for wanting Mama to stop saying the room was there. To stop believing in it. I'd get up from the roof and brush the black dust off my bare knees.

And time did pass, just like we wanted it to. And I left, went out on my own and worked a day job and took classes at night, and I did well, I was always good in school, and then I got my MPH in another night program, it took a few years, and I ended up—in one of the mountain buildings, in my own little place, with my beige sofa, my good table and chairs, my green Chinese rug. Looking out my western window (I don't rate a lake view) right over the city toward where I grew up. I haven't been out there for fifteen years. Under the fading sky after I've watched the sunset, I imagine all of us, back then, the way, back then, I imagined the secret room that I actually come home to now. The only one of us I find, when I get here, is me. Thinking of Mama holding Bobo, and Zulie and Jean, and Desmond and Donald, and me too, once upon a time, all of us getting on each other's nerves and making a lot of noise and just doing what people do, living day by day in that old way, maybe wishing for, maybe imagining, and willing to give anything for some room they can't see and can't find that would make life so much better, sometimes I feel like—on the other side of which wall of mine is the imaginary room of what really did happen?

ON SAD SUBURBAN AFTERNOONS
OF AUTUMN

On sad suburban afternoons of autumn,
       the piercings, leather, and tattoos that bought
these bungalows from mixing bowls and golf
       barbecue and drink beer, watch football, eat,
laugh like ponies—everything has changed
       and not a lot except which music blares
through the meat-scented smoke and streaks of sun.
       Big motorcycles drip dark staining oil
where Oldsmobiles once waited between breakdowns.
       Slightly aslant on windows are the self-
adhesive souvenirs of stadium concerts
       by rockers getting osteoporosis;
T-shirts advertise five-pointed leaves;
       kids are neglected in the age-old ways,
unkempt and shrieking as they run—or older,
       buy their own weed, sneak drinks, ditch school and fuck.
In front yards, back yards, alleys and dead ends
       may all these signs convince the distant gods—
or Fate, or The Fates, an absent "G-d," a Christ
       somewhere or other, not right here, an Allah
with gnashing prophets, or a great magician,
       or the chance events that can destroy a life—
that there's no need to bring down any more
       than customary miseries and brief
illusions of good luck on such old, young,
       different, same, frail creatures of a day.

BROADWAY & ARGYLE

after Wang Wei

Smoky, cold, broken late-afternoon clouds
        mob eastward. Walking west, I see on side-
walks no one I know, no one who knows me,
        yet from all our wandering at this same
hour come shared underthoughts we can hear. Then
        once again that which is not darkness un-
darkens our obscurity, slants rightly
        from sky to make bleak slush-ice meekly gleam.

SLOW MOTION

There was this guy at one of the pay phones, saying, "Yes, sweetie, what do you feel about that? Were you scared at the way Mommy was talking?" You could hear his voice all over that corner of the lobby. My job, you know, you don't have to make any effort at compassion when you work with a machine. If it isn't doing its job, it's not because something bad happened to it. This guy's voice was tender; also full of resignation that he couldn't change whatever was going on at the other end of the line. He said, "I'm going to be home the day after tomorrow, do you think you can get yourself ready for bed tonight, and then get up and go to school tomorrow, because then I'll be home the next day, OK?" Dealing with even a smart machine, like this one, is a blessing. And if it's down, that's even better, that can be a gift from the company, at least as far as I'm concerned. The man was saying, "Mommy is very tired, and she needs to be alone for a while, can you get ready for bed by yourself?" He pulled on his cigarette deep enough to suck the smoke all the way down into his legs, and then, while he was stubbing it out in the ashtray, he said, "I know you don't want to, but you can do it, you're a big girl now." The room reservations for the next million years are in this thing's memory, along with credit card numbers, phone numbers, addresses, company names, titles, all kinds of stuff beyond that. Running a batch of updates for tomorrow, if you know what to do and you aren't frightened by machines like this, is a piece of cake. The guy looked at his watch, it was almost eleven p.m. here, he crumpled his empty pack and tossed it at the trash can and missed. He was listening a long time. The only other person at the desk with me was Heather, poking along. I have this problem with her—I have it with everybody. "What *did* you want to eat for dinner? Did you want a peanut butter sandwich like I make for you?" He started fishing around in his briefcase and he found another pack of cigarettes and tore it open while he held the phone in the crook of his neck; he tapped the first few a little bit out of the pack and took one with his lips and lit it with a match from a hotel matchbook beside the ashtray. My problem especially with Heather but with everybody, and I can't help this, this is just the way I am, I don't do any drugs or anything, is that I'm always waiting on them to catch up to me. Everything else is in like slow motion for me, everything but me: I'm in real time and everyone else is going really, really slow. The guy moves the phone from one hand to the other, from one side of his neck to the other, as he gets out of his suit coat one arm at a time and folds it and lays it over his briefcase, which is standing on the floor, now, and he's still listening. Then he said, "Yes, honey, I know you felt bad, I know you were worried, but you don't have to worry, Daddy doesn't want you to worry, everything is OK, you can go to sleep and have happy dreams, and then go to school tomorrow, and Daddy will be home the next day." I run a routine on the computer while I'm showing Heather or somebody else how to do it and they just can't get it, and I'm supposed to show them how to do it so that I don't have to be the one to do it, I'm supposed to be troubleshooting, not doing the daily procedures. But for me it ends up being easier just to do it—faster, I mean, a lot faster, than it would be for me to go over it again and again and then have the staff change and me start over again with somebody new. "Honey?" the man said, "You need to go to bed, now, sweetie, it's time to go to bed—where's Mommy now?" He looked pretty sad. My mother was crazy, and that's no lie—she had to be as crazy as that guy's wife. When I was eleven years old she went about two months of that year without speaking to anyone in the family: so withdrawn from me, my sister, and my father that we almost got used to her that way, and we would talk about her when she was standing right beside us because since she wasn't saying anything to anyone it was like she *wasn't* there; like she had gone somewhere; like not only did she not speak to us, but we didn't see her. The man said, "I'm going to send you a big kiss, through the telephone, OK?" He stubbed his cigarette out and exhaled a cloud of smoke, slow. "I'm going to send you a kiss, are you ready?" She didn't even talk on the phone to other people, and we were having to say, week after week, that she couldn't come to the phone or was out or was asleep. She came back to us, that time, when her old boss happened to call, and I went ahead and asked her, as we always did, while I covered the phone with the palm of my other hand, did she want to talk to him, and she surprised me by coming up and taking the phone—he had called to offer her her job back, after she'd been home more than a year because the strain had been too much for her—but she was a good secretary and he wanted her back, he was willing to have her, crazy and all (and I was amazed to be hearing her voice again; I had forgotten it, almost, forgotten what it was like when she did talk: I liked to hear her voice, but there was something in it that I never got, that she never gave to me, and maybe she didn't give it to anyone, but you could hear it, hiding inside there, teasing you, not coming out all the way, when you heard her talk the way she did that night to her old boss). "Here it comes!" the man said on the phone,

"Here comes the kiss, are you ready?" He listened a few seconds and he said, "Are you ready?" I couldn't concentrate. I couldn't do what I was supposed to do, and Heather was down the counter from me hopelessly lost in something or other she was probably screwing up, reservations or receipts or whatever, I didn't know and didn't care. He said, "Here it comes!" and he made a really loud kissing sound with his lips. "Did you get it?" he said. He had a huge smile on his face to make his voice sound cheerful to her, but she must have been crying, and he didn't say anything but just held the phone to his ear for a while, listening to her, or maybe listening to the dial tone because she had hung up or had the phone hung up for her or who knows, but his face wasn't smiling anymore. I bailed out of my program and set the system back to ready, and I felt like I had to let my hands hang straight down, like I couldn't really raise my arms up. I remember doing that—just listening after the other person has hung up already. I've seen the inside of some hospitals in my time, the day rooms with everyone in pajamas reeking of cigarettes and their hair all goofus and the loud TVs—I *worked* in a hospital once, jeez, but in data processing, where I never had to deal with a patient. The man put his elbows up on the narrow marble telephone counter, and put his face in his hands. He didn't care what other people saw. I was feeling jumpy and like everybody else was in slo-mo. I had about six more hours to kill on my shift, and—although I have an excellent memory for just about everything, a really unusual memory that is not in every way a blessing, let me tell you—I couldn't say now how I spent them.

SPARROW

In the town streets
pieces of the perishing world
Pieces of the world coming into being

The peculiar angle at which a failing gutter descends
from a house-eave; a squirrel's surviving tattered nest of leaves
woven into a high bare crook of an elm tree
    (the last one alive on this street)

The small bright green leafing out of that elm
A man shaking coins in a dry Coke-cup and saying
Small change, brother? Small change?
                  A woman
in scuffed white running shoes and a fine suit hurrying
down the street with a baggy briefcase that must have
papers and her purse and her good shoes inside it
Perhaps a small pistol

Gusts rattle the half-closed upstairs window
    in the old office building that's going to be torn down

Skittering across the sidewalk, a scrap of paper
    with someone's handwriting on it, in pencil
A message that will arrive

Things in themselves

A few minutes of seeing
An exalting

Or a few minutes of complete shelter
A protectedness, a brief rest from the changes

Sparrow moments

|||||||

But this emblem I take from the world—
able, fussing, competing
at the feeder, waiting on a branch,
sudden in flight, looping and rushing, to another branch,
quick to fight over mating and quick at mating,
surviving winter on dry dead seed-heads of weeds
and around stables and garbage and park benches,
near farms and in deep woods,
brooding in summer-hidden nests—house sparrow,

song sparrow, fox sparrow, swamp sparrow,
field sparrow, lark sparrow, tree sparrow, sage sparrow,
white-throated sparrow of the falling whistled song
that I hear as a small reassurance—

Would my happiness be that the sparrow not be emblem—
that it be only in my mind as it is outside of my mind, itself,
that my mind not remove it from itself
into realms of forms and symbolic thinking?

My happiness, that is, my best being

Words like branches and leaves,
or words like the birds among
the branches and leaves?

They take wing all at once
The way they flee makes flight look like exuberance not fear
They veer away around a house-corner.

AN ACHING YOUNG MAN

An aching young
            man on the street
approaches, stops
            me with his eyes
and saying Sir?
            Sir? he shows me
his right hand, it's
            purple and red,
blood-spotted, gro-
            tesquely swollen,
he says he fell
            while chasing a
thief who'd grabbed his
            backpack, with his
wallet in it,
            he has to get
home by bus to
            Carbondale, he
needs sixty-five
            dollars, he has
fifty, he shows
            me, his jaw moves,
What about the
            emergency
room? I ask, Man,
            he says, I don't
have a thousand
            for that bill, What
about pain pills,
            Advil, something?
I ask, he says
            That's eight dollars
for a bottle
            right there, he is
pressing his left
            thumb deep into

the soft water-
                balloon scabbing
mess of his harmed
                right hand, he says
Man, this hurts, it
                feels better when
I press on it,
                Don't do that, I
say, but I don't
                know anything,
why do I say
                it except his
hand looks so bad
                I don't see how
he'll recover?—
                A nurse, he says,
she told me if
                it's this swollen
then it isn't
                broken it's frac-
tured You know what
                time it is?—in
the face of his
                logic I hold
out no alter-
                natives, I hold
up my unharmed
                right hand to show
him my watch, he
                says, I can't see
it, and I tell
                him it's two, I
ask myself why
                can't he see it?
and he says My
                bus is at five
then I live an
                hour and a half

on the other
                side of that Got
to get back to
                Kentucky, while
a nearby bill-
                board keeps showing
us both an ad,
                a visage half
woman and half
                leopard, a face
this age wrongly
                puts on fortune,
maybe, wronging
                the woman, the
leopard, and us,
                and in the row
of courageous
                trees that live and
die down the side-
                walk, a wind is
shoving the leaves
                this way and that.

OH

In summer breezes the leaves of the old trees shake.
On the gentle slope the shaded sidewalks are dry.
Under the August afternoon the lake
Answers with both gray and blue the clouds and sky.

I amble along, one hundred years ago
(When with hand tools the house where I live was built)
Till a small poem—shape of both id and ego—
Arrives at the end of a wandering, walking thought.

Immediately the poem feels vertigo, it moves
With a hitch in its gait, it's not convinced it should have been
Given this path, when it would have liked to discover
An unforeseen matriarch or a vague feather or a violin.

At land's edge, tumbled defenses of dumped rocks,
The size of sealed crates and graffiti'd with odd codes
For the strange destinations that they'll never reach,
Till now have kept the lake from the land it erodes

And the land from throwing itself once and for all
Into the lake on an impulse it could no longer suppress.
And the one-hundred-year-old poem, taller on formerly metrical
Tiptoes than the highest rock, scans the horizon for rescue

From this world into which it was born by mistake.
I do not imagine swans flying away for all time
But the town disappearing by winter (while the poem was still
        trying to make
Sense, poor thing) and scavenger gulls that feed on rhyme.

BOY ON A BUSY CORNER

Arriving from some station with his one bag,
an alligator-plastic cardboard suitcase

of a sort to raise pity
when I look back at him after walking by,

here he has come, we all know, uncounted times over the decades,
speaking to himself silently, trying not to turn his head so violently

to follow what he sees, and walking marked by awe
on the streets of the city strugglers, so visibly

unlike them yet already becoming at least a little
like them, not in success (even if only the success of

simply living in the city) but in the burdens of knowing
their disappointments, their sustained unrealized plans,

their stance and gait of anxiousness or hurry or
determined nonchalance, the city

style, the shoes and coats and clasping of the hands
of their children for whom enough could not be provided,

from whom disappointment could not long be held off
outside the great store windows, far below the old

office ledges, the new glass parapets, and what he does not yet know of:
the copied documents and bills of lading, the gleaming tray

of cool dry crystal flutes ready for champagne in the boardroom,
the tired, uninvited reps elevatoring down thirty or fifty floors

to make at least one more call, the pharaonic lobby
with presiding guard and metonymical directory.

Everything he sees and hears is a first amazement
in the midst of the only half-crowded streets, especially

the guitar-playing blues singer whose mojo is always working,
her howling mutt right with her, and that unforgettable scar on her forehead.

Some knowledge returned to me that I had stood here,
that I was here before I ever arrived, or he, and then did arrive.

That I came as, I came in, every earlier incarnation of every desire
to arrive, to have come to a center of things,

where possibilities could not be counted on
the fingers of even two hands if they really were possible.

Here he was, leaning out, looking up the wide noisy streets
that lie deep between big stone, big steel, buildings, a boy,

a young man, on his own, not yet knowing those things that I need
to know, perhaps able to stop dreaming, to understand,

to assess fully, to hope yet to hold back his invisible horse,
to find for himself some work, some friend, some beautiful girl.

A MAN IN A SUIT

Very late last night, a warm spring evening, a greenish blue raft of ectoplasm came amoebaing across the parking lot, nobody saw from where. And when it got near the door of the Clark St. 24-hour Jewel-Osco, where the light just pours out of that place, it brightened up a bit, and people standing around were pretty fascinated but not wanting it to get too close to them, only a couple of them ran off in a fright. This thing seethed toward its center—it was about the size of a queen-size mattress—and up into the air it slowly lifted a column of itself, I guess I would say, that turned into the figure of a man in a tan poplin suit, white shirt, no tie, I can't say if it was really a man. With skin halfway between white and black, by which I mean both pink and brown, and wearing very dark sunglasses. So he floated to the edge of the ectoplasm and stepped out of it onto the asphalt like he was stepping out of mud, and he nodded to one man who was nearby—not a friendly greeting but the kind of nod that one man will give another to signal that there is truce between them, no cause for alarm or action, or any feeling whatsoever, for that matter—and then the man, if like I said it was a man, when he got closer to the entrance he triggered the automatic door open, just like anybody else would do, and he went inside.

There are always lots of shoppers in this particular Jewel-Osco, even late at night. (Maybe in every Jewel-Osco—this place knows how to make money.) Some of the shoppers in the lot hung around the ectoplasmic raft and several others followed the man inside and watched him take a cart and go first to the pharmacy section and get some cold remedy and some chewable vitamin C, and then pick up a couple of ballpoint pens and a legal pad and a roll of Scotch Magic Tape from the school-supply section, and then head into the groceries, where he bought biscuit mix, corn flakes, a jar of red raspberry jelly, a pound of bacon, a pound of drip-grind coffee and some no. 6 filters, a half gallon of orange juice in a carton, and a dozen farm-fresh, free-range brown eggs, grade AA, extra large.

People said he did not react to any other person in the store. Never seemed to look at anybody. Some said that if you were standing where he walked by, or you were near him in the checkout line, there was that chemical smell of something brand-new around him, like there is with a new shower curtain.

This man was a very patient person—he was at the register of the check-out girl who only started yesterday. His bill was $19.92. He paid with regular used-looking U.S. cash money. He asked for plastic not paper. The bagger handed him his bag and afterward, when he found out who, or maybe what, his customer had been, he said that when his fingers touched the man's, they felt just like ordinary fingers to him. The man never once took off his sunglasses. He was trim, somewhat tall, and reasonably clean looking.

By now there was a pretty large crowd outside around the ectoplasmic puddle. It was bubbling once in a while, and it kind of quivered and throbbed somewhat around the edges. It had a very peculiar smell, like a combination of burnt hair and ozone gas from off an electrical appliance. And it might as well have been a trained pet, it was waiting so faithfully for the man, not leaving its spot by the automatic doors, despite all the attention being paid to it by the crowd of people jammed around it to get a look but staying several feet away so as not to be touched by it. It didn't respond to anything anybody said to it, although several people tried talking to it, and shouting to it, like it might be able to hear but not very well. It was only about half a foot thick, but it was more than that in the middle, where the man had come out of it.

Then here came the man again out through the automatic doors. People fell back from him as he came out carrying his plastic bag of groceries, wearing that pretty nice suit, and nicely pressed, too. He was now wearing a hat, the old-fashioned kind that men wore in movies—which everyone said was not on him when he went into the store, when he did his shopping, or when he paid for his groceries. No one else in the store was even wearing a suit.

He nodded to a few men, the way he had before, and without looking at any of the women (one of them screamed, just a little). And somebody said the police were on the way, but it had been by my estimate fifteen minutes since they had been called (by me), and they hadn't showed up yet.

The man came to the edge of the blue-green raft of ectoplasm and stepped into it and sank right through it and disappeared into it with his shopping bag like it was the surface of a deep swimming pool filled with opaque ink and the ectoplasmic substance rose in a thick lump of almost a splash where he had gone through it, and a little whiff of vapor came off the lump like a tiny cloud. Several people said it smelled like a locker room; others who were directly in its path as it drifted a few yards and evaporated said that it had no smell at all; and there were yet a few more who said it had that burnt hair/ozone scent to it.

As soon as the man in the suit had gone into the raft of ectoplasm, it gathered itself somewhat and began to bubble more and extend its way back into the parking lot, with people on that side jumping out of its way as soon as they saw it was coming at them. Nobody seemed to really be afraid of it, it just didn't feel that way, they said when I spoke with them afterward. But they sure didn't want it to touch them. On the spot where it had been waiting, it left behind the plastic bag, but it was empty, although the cash register receipt was still in it. Some shoppers trailed after the ectoplasm. A lot did, and yet nobody ever said what else it did or what happened to it, that I could find out.

Probably a lot of people will say they were there and saw it, but there were at most thirty, and some of them were too scared to catch more than a glimpse of it. There is a DJ for one of the rock stations who said this morning on the air that this had all been staged by his station, but he would not reveal how or what for. The TV Action Eyewitness News van <u>was</u> there but came too late to get anything on video except the spot where the ecto had stayed waiting for its man, and the empty recyclable grocery bag with the receipt inside. They wanted to measure the exact distance of the bag from the automatic doors, but the bag had started drifting with the breeze as soon as the ecto let go of it.

Maybe it was the man that was the faithful pet of this thing, and it sent him on an errand for it, to bring it the fixings for breakfast. I believe it was hungry. Maybe there wasn't any man at all and what people thought was a man was only a remote-control part of itself that the queen-size mattress of ectoplasm sent into the Jewel-Osco in that shape so that it could shop like a person and pay for things the way anybody else would do.

There was a little bit of a run on the Osco liquor department afterward, but no problems. Very little additional to add (but I would like to add that I am pleased to have prepared this report and if Director Johnson would like reports on a regular basis, I would be happy to take care of that. I always have liked writing.) A local patrol car showed up about two hours after the incident, and it was real apparent that they were not interested. One copy of this report has been sent to Director Johnson, one to the store manager, Jim Lanuzzi, and one to a man who asked for it and left his name and address, who said he was studying neighborhood dynamics on Clark St., which I did not see any harm in doing, at this point.

Jerry Wozcik
Night Security Group Captain, 1/27/92

HUNGRY MAN RAIDS SUPERMARKET

The carts, half-filled and abandoned
for the moment, were strewn in the aisles
like some small riverside derailment
and a woman turned, looked
at me, cold streams fell
into the pit of my stomach,
she put her arm across
her son's shoulders—quickly—
and pulled him out of my path:
a boy whose face was hers
though in him the timidity was
less from fright than from
plainness and innocence, he didn't
smile upward at me like a supplicant
the way she did, from the shallows.
Already I had a sense
of having waded into myself
till I was up to my own hands
and the undertow pulling at me.
Her look made me recognize the deeps
into which I was stepping,
where the water came almost
to my mouth.
                    It wasn't the boy
I wanted, she didn't need
to shield him from me.
What story rising in her,
that she wouldn't tell perhaps
ever to anyone, led her
to such a fear for her child,
the premonitions rushing
at her all at once?

The water flowed by
under the overhanging trees,
mother and son stood beyond

the wrecked sleeping cars
in a little eddy to one side
and the boy looked up at her
for an answer but she had none,
it wasn't something she could explain to him—
her panic at seeing the man
who had stood near them, there,
at the place where they were
without husband or father,
then his stepping off into the hidden
suck-hole in the middle
(did he think he was going
to save some lives?) and not
coming up again . . .

And now the stranger was gone
into the cold pool of himself
the way a man will do,
where water closed over him
and the current spun down
into a point far from mothers and sons.
The danger was past,
they went on without him
down cold-lit store aisles again,
without what he would have told them
and without finding in themselves
what they would have had to tell.

THE BLUE DRESS

You tore it off my back.

But I'm not good
at telling a story—you'd shut
me up by saying that—
so I guess I can't tell this one,
that had to do with the way
I once used to feel
when someone like you
who had done a rough kind
of work—work that can kill you
if you're not careful—talked
to me like my listening
was important to him.
                          And listened
to me, too, made me feel
I could be the gentleness
he needed after bad
times—someone who'd grown
up hard and alone, like you,
or gotten through the war
alive . . . But I don't feel
the same about you any-
more, or nearly anyone,
any man, I've known.
I thought when I met you
and it was exciting to me
to be with you, it was
more life I was getting—
but it was less.

But you said I was special,
I was the best of all
the girls—the women—you'd had,
the sexiest, I turned you on
the most. That's what I'd

remember when I'd want
to leave you, when you'd been
after me again, like always
drunk, hunting me or saying
you'd kill me. I'd try remembering
that nobody else ever told me
I was special or beautiful,
and I thought it was loving
me that made you say it—
I know I'm not pretty
the way some women are,
the way some were that you
would look at twice and make
me forget what you'd done
and want you for myself again.

But it was just being
scared that kept me from leaving,
you saw to that many times.
And I did used to love you,
I did love your kisses,
love that touch you had for me,
holding my face in your hands,
squeezing my shoulders for me,
the way you'd rub my tired legs
and how you'd put your hands
on my breasts, that was so careful,
I thought, not to hurt.
And my gripping you as hard
to me as I could, and you'd
say I was the best of all
of them, the best and the best
till the waves of it hit—
I'd float for a long
second or two and then it
slams through, so sweet.

But you'd hit me. Just sitting
together in the apartment and you'd
jump up and hit me yelling
"Don't do that!" and I don't
even know what it is.
You used your belt on me,
you threw me down the stairs
more than once and locked
me out alone for hours
and I never knew anyone
in the building who I could
go to, I'd just stay down
near the front door inside,
people would come in and go out
and hold the door for me
but I'd say no, I was
waiting for someone. . . .

Till you came down to look.
When you made up to me
I was so happy to have
you back—back to yourself—
and we'd go out dancing,
you'd know everybody there
and those friends of yours would always
pretend that nothing's wrong.
I felt grateful to them
for treating me so friendly,
so polite, so respectful. Nice.
And they could laugh with me,
in a way you couldn't, or wouldn't.

The preacher says to talk.
So I do and he listens
and doesn't say very much.
He still thinks that all
the bad came from you, that
everything bad that was done,

you did—which I'm not going
to tell him any different.
All he knows about that
night is you chased me
downstairs and into the street
at 3 a.m. with me
in my nightgown in the cold and no shoes
and you with the sharp kitchen
knife in your hand, yelling
you were going to cut me.

You never even knew how
afraid I was to go
to sleep and afraid to wait up
for you, too, but what would
you have cared, in those moods—
I went crazy wondering
what you'd do when you came in,
turning like a mean dog
and trying to get me when you
could barely stand up and had
to hold onto the furniture
to walk across the room.

I don't know how you
were able all of a sudden
to move so fast that night,
the state you were in, and the knife
in your hand. Then when you stopped
in the middle of the dead
street and said it was over
and turned around and started
back, I don't know why
I followed you home, either.

I watched you real carefully
when you got into bed
with your clothes on and you put

the knife under your pillow
and said to me that if I
wanted to kill you while you
were sleeping, there it was.

I waited one more hour
watching the clock go slow,
afraid you'd wake up
sick out of your alcohol sleep
and with one of your nightmares.
Then I had to reach under
your pillow to find the knife
and I cut my finger on it—
I almost cried out
but I realized that what I was
was so mad at you that
all of a sudden I wanted
to beat you hard as I could
with my fists and scream and it
still makes me crazy and I
wish I had done it—
instead. But I didn't
make a sound, just held
my cut finger that I couldn't
look at and looked at you
for a long time, trying
to guess where in you was your heart.

I had a thought and I
went back to the kitchen to put
a bandage on my cut and hold
it till it stopped bleeding
and only throbbed and I called
the police. Come over here
right now, I told them, I'm
going to kill him, and I gave
the address, the apartment,
the floor, the bedroom. . . . I wanted

a bunch of them in case
they had to save me from
what you might do while you
were dying.
            Or maybe what
I wanted was what they did.

I took the knife and went
first to unlock the door
for when they'd come, wondering
how long it would be. I stood
in the doorway to our room
counting to two hundred
in my mind and then counted
again, and heard them stamping
and running up the stairs
so loud I thought they'd wake you
and I ran to stab your chest
holding the knife with both hands.

It slipped sideways and tore
your shirt down your ribs
and only cut you some.
You jumped and opened your eyes
but it didn't seem like you
could see me and I stabbed you
again and it slipped again,
I couldn't make it go
into you, but too late to stop.

When the cops pulled you off
of me—I don't know where
the knife went—know what?
I had to run onto the back
landing outside and pull
the door shut, that always
locks, lock myself out
because you were yelling

Help me, Esther, help me
please God Esther, help,
they're killing me, Esther!
I would have rushed back
and killed those cops to get
them off of you.

Then the noise was gone away.
I was trying to figure out
how to get back in, freezing
and crying in my nightgown,
they must have taken you away
and what would happen to you
and how could I get you out
somehow when I heard two shots
from the street around front.
I don't know what they've said
you did—when they came up
calling for me and let me
into our place and told me
what had happened to you
I couldn't seem to hear them.

What I thought of while they
were talking and talking and waiting
for me to say something
that I wasn't going to say
was how I'd last seen one
of them at your back holding
you by the collar the way
you grabbed mine the night
you tore my new blue dress
that you couldn't tell from silk
right off my back, left me
naked in a corner with my hands
up and you yelling at me
I spent too much of your money,
said I wouldn't leave you alone,

made me get in the closet
and locked me in there, shouted
through the door if I ever
tried to leave you, you would
cut me so bad, no one
would want me, while I cried
into a torn rag of my dress,
all ruined and lost and wasted.

That was for you, that dress,
to make you happy, make
you want to be with me.
All I had was a physical
need in my body, for you,
and wanting you to say
you loved me and be nice
the way you used to be.
I kept thinking that if
I was nicer to you
you'd get better, you'd be
all right again, and I'd
be special to you, like before.
Now nothing can change ever
between us, we'll always
be stuck where we were that night.
Only I'm the only one
to feel it, you can't.

The preacher will tell me I
should forgive you now,
should let it go, should come
to church once in a while,
I look at him and see
another man looking at me.
You used to tell all your
stories to your friends, the hard
knocks you'd had—you said
harder than mine. Is this

story good enough, you think,
for me to tell it? But you
aren't listening, you can't
answer me, you never did,
you're not here but you won't
go away, and you can't
give me back what you took
if you're dead. If you could
give me back that one dress
then you could give me everything,
even the way one time you put
your hand in my hair after
you had hit me and said
Please don't cry, sugar, don't,
honey, stop crying, please,
I promise to you that
I'll never do it ever again.

THE AFFECT OF ELMS

Across the narrow street from the old hotel that now
houses human damage temporarily—
deranged, debilitated, but up and around in their odd
postures, taking their meds, or maybe trading them—

is the little park, once a neighboring mansion's side yard,
where beautiful huge old elm trees, long in that place,
stand in a close group over the mown green lawn
watered and well kept by the city, their shapes expressive:

the affect of elms is of struggle upward and survival,
of strength—despite past grief (the bowed languorous arches)
and torment (limbs in the last stopped attitude of writhing)—

while under them wander the deformed and tentative
persons, accompanied by voices, counting their footsteps,
exhaling the very breath the trees breathe in.

RED LINE HOWARD/95TH

Settin' in the house with everything on my mind
Settin' in the house with everything on my mind
Lookin' at the clock and can't even tell the time
    —Bessie Smith

The newspaper classified ad said: I will

restring the old beads or pearls

that you have set aside a while ago.

I don't think that everbody will come back

to work that workt there, in the stil industry.

No I don't think they can.

Another said: Have 5 pit bull puppies

three girls and two boys one of the girls

is deaf she has her shots I have pictures

My mama said I was a quiet child

My mama said I was a real quiet child

Didn't know I would grow up so wild

That man liked doing things for his wife

finding things to do for his wife

but like it was for who she'd been in some other life

And another said: Cemetery Lots.
6 Beverly cemetery lots in Jewish
section, singles or multiples.

And another one said: Baby's christening
gown, its hand made crocheted of
tiniest white thread, completely lace $20

Mother and Dad, the second time
they married each other was in 1946
in Beaumont, Texas, then they come up here.

The boozhwazee I don't entirely understand
The boozhwazee I think I do understand
And I know what it means when they give me the back of they hand.

State Street's all right and lights shine nice and bright
State Street's all right and lights shine nice and bright
But I'd rather be in Bessemer reading by a candle light
    —Ma Rainey

MISSION

After she had been in her first school for months already, one afternoon at home she was crying because of something a friend had done or maybe only said to her, and I was trying to offer some solace, some distraction, when she nearly shouted all of a sudden, "You and Mommy left without even saying goodbye to me!" I said—shocked to have caused a wound so lingering that other pain must inevitably lead back to it—"When?"

"The first day of kindergarten," she said, and she really began to wail, looking up at the ceiling, tears pouring from her, her face crumpling.

"But you wanted us to leave! You were lined up with the other kids to go into class behind the teacher, I thought you were happy to go in!"

"But the other parents were still there! And you left without even saying goodbye!" she said. The way rain can arrive with a violent flurry of pouring and thunder but then settles into a steady fall that is the real rain, that will after a while flood gutters and basements and streets and fields and rivers till there's damage it will take time to repair—so she settled wearily and deeply into her crying.

However a wound was caused, it is already there, and it can't be undone, it needs to be healed.

My child is standing before me on the steps down to the back door, her eyes level with mine as I sit on a higher step holding both her hands, and she is crying as if she will never stop, and the friend's slight is forgotten, the first day of kindergarten is forgotten, there is deeper sorrow than that, incomprehensible and punishing, and for now I am pouring over her the unslakeable longing and helpless protective presentiment that bind me irremediably to her in love, and I understand again what I must do as long as she and I live, and how much I want to do this, to love her, and need to, and how too it is not enough. It is in the way of things, and no blame on anyone for it, that it is not enough.

RICH PALE PINK

Rich pale pink and
                    peach, clear like
watercolor
                    washes, or
glowing thick on
                    the lumpy
undersides of
                    clouds against
dry widening blue
                    of eastern
sky at late-March
                    dawn, begin-
ning to reveal
                    gray streets, roofs
gray, blue-gray, brown,
                    and inter-
laced bare top elm
                    branches, sun-
light arrives; at
                    dusk, like a
delayed visual
                    answer that's
been pondered for
                    ten hours, come
the same colors,
                    but different
feelings, as rich
                    streaks peach, pink,
orange, crimson,
                    against cold
withdrawing blue.
                    I praise this
spectacle that
                    makes me small
at our two back-
                    of-the-house

upstairs windows,
                through which in
silence I can
                ponder the
empty yards of
                our neighbors—
ordinary
                dignity
of daily life
                scruffily
perfected by
                the absence
of everyone,
                the dead cars,
toys lying side-
                ways for a
season, a child's
                cap flung down
this afternoon,
                all at once
the day has passed,
                they're home now
from work, school, play,
                everyone
whom we missed or
                who is hurt-
ing us is here
                or absent,
supper is brought
                from ancient
kitchens, the night
                sky, cloudy
or clear, bears off
                its losses,
lets its bright spheres
                glow, withstands
our unconscious-
                ness of them.

FRIDAY SNOW

Something needs to be done—like dragging a big black plastic sack through the upstairs rooms, emptying into it each wastebasket, the trash of three lives for a week or so. I am careful and slow about it, so that this little chore will banish the big ones. But I leave the bag lying on the floor and I go into my daughter's bedroom, into the north morning light from her windows, and while this minute she is at school counting or spelling a first useful word I sit down on her unmade bed and I look out the windows at nothing for a while, the unmoving buildings—houses and a church—in the cold street.

Across it a dark young man is coming slowly down the white sidewalk with a snow shovel over his shoulder. He's wearing only a light coat, there's a plastic shower cap under his navy blue knit hat, and at a house where the walk hasn't been cleared he climbs the steps and rings the doorbell and stands waiting, squinting sideways at the wind. Then he says a few words I can't hear to the storm door that doesn't open, and he nods his head with the kindly farewell that is a habit he wears as a disguise, and he goes back down the steps and on to the next house. All of this in pantomime, the way I see it through windows closed against winter and the faint sounds of winter.

My daughter's cross-eyed piggy bank is also staring out blankly, and in its belly are four dollar bills that came one at a time from her grandmother and which tomorrow she will pull out of the corked-mouth-hole. (It's not like the piggy banks you have to fill before you empty them because to empty them you have to smash them.) Tomorrow she will buy a perfect piece of small furniture for her warm well-lit dollhouse where no one is tired or weak and the wind can't get in.

Sitting on her bed, looking out, I didn't see the lame neighbor child, bundled-up and out of school or even turned out of the house for a while, or the blind woman with burns or the sick veteran—people who might have walked past, stoop-shouldered with what's happened and will keep happening to them. So much limping is not from physical pain—the pain is gone now, but the leg's still crooked. The piggy bank and I see only the able young man whose straight back nobody needs.

When he finally gets past where I can see him, it feels as if a kind of music has stopped, and it's more completely quiet than it was, an emptiness more than a stillness, and I get up from the rumpled bed and smooth the covers, slowly and carefully, and look around the room for something to pick up or straighten, and take a wadded dollar bill from my pocket and put it into the pig, and walk out.

NONNA

There was a little wooden shack built into the very colonnade itself at one end—a long colonnade of thick, tall Ionic columns that ran along the back of the mansion. And there was a thin young uniformed but unshaven doorman walking slowly up and down among the columns. Not the real doorman, just an underling to keep watch over the back of the mansion, because it stood in the crowded city, and the large gardens, although walled, were nonetheless open to all because the wall had fallen in places, leaving wide gaps. And the iron back gate itself, from which she had a close clear view of the colonnade and the shack, was fully open, leaning at an angle, and grass and weeds were growing around it.

When the rear doorman was at the far end of the colonnade, she went as fast as she could through the gate and up two huge marble steps that took every bit of her strength—and to the shack, and tried the door. This was a miraculous find, in this part of the city where she had never been before: the door was not locked. She quickly pushed in and closed it stealthily behind her, and sat down on the floor with her back to it.

While she waited to see how safe this would turn out to be, she looked around her. There was a window—with the panes still in it!—on the side that faced away from the doorman, so through it she could see overgrown hedges nearby. The shack was all unpainted inside, but quite sound. Built out from the rough walls with bare unpainted planks were a little stool, a single shelf, and a small table. And there were *two* roofs!—the roof of the shack, and outside of it, far above it, the slate roof of the colonnade.

This was very satisfactory. She must keep it the greatest secret. And she would be well situated for as long as she could stay hidden from that doorman, who surely was not on duty all day and night. It shouldn't be hard to learn his routine—she could sit and wait a long time to learn it, if need be.

After a while she grew more comfortable, more self-possessed, more in possession of the place. It was warm enough inside for her, since she didn't intend to take off her coats. She even slept a tiny bit—but watchfully, warily, ready to defend her home against that doorman.

Then the door was shoved against her back and she fell to one side and had to struggle to right herself again, and she tried to push back, angrily. But she didn't have enough strength to resist the force from the other side.

It was the doorman, grinning malevolently at her. "Did you think I didn't see you come in here?" he said softly. From the loose heap of herself on the floor, looking up at him in his gray overcoat with a blue stripe, his blue hat, she did not answer him, and set her mouth in a snarl.

"I saw you," he said. "Get out of here!" he shouted. "This isn't some place where you can sleep. You can't start living here! Get out!" And he pulled his open hand back as if he would slap her. She cringed a bit, and as slowly as she could, she worked against him by pretending to look around her for the things she didn't have, pretending to gather herself till she could stand.

He caught her by one arm and pulled her up, but the sleeve slipped off her arm in the process, and from her eyes a few tears ran down her cheeks. They were not from pain, or from fear of what he might do, but because she was losing this grand place, this best place she had ever found, because of him. This could have been a little place just for her, not big enough for anyone else, perfect because she didn't want anyone else. But of course it was too good, nobody would ever get to use it, it was wasted, at the back of this huge house. He pulled her out the door—not quite slowly enough— and down the two huge steps, where she nearly toppled, to the lawn, and let go of her. "You can't use that to stay in, no one is allowed to stay there," he said to her sardonically. He pulled his hand back again as if really to slap her this time, as she was struggling to get her arm back into that one sleeve, which kept escaping her, she couldn't get it, and she had to get it before she could take another step, she had to catch that sleeve and get her arm into it before she did anything else, even speak.

"Hey! What are you doing!" a man's voice called out. She and the doorman, both astonished, turned toward the gate, where a well-dressed, middle-aged man was standing, watching. "Are you going to hit that old woman?" he called out, his tone challenging, authoritative.

The doorman slowly let his arm fall to his side. "This is a private house, no one is allowed into these gardens," he said, in a more dignified voice, one that perhaps he was practicing for his future turn at the front of the house.

His warning, his right to hold his ground against anyone not of the household, no matter who he was, did nothing to stop the well-dressed man, who stepped swiftly into the back yard and looked down into the face of the woman, and, at last, kindly held for her the sleeve that she hadn't been able to capture, and guided her arm into it. She pulled the outer coat closed in front of her, grasping it tightly, and looked up at the men, each in turn.

"You have no right to treat this woman that way, you little creep," the man said. He was larger than the scrawny doorman, who said nothing, but found the nerve to grin at this interloper. "Good," he said. "She's all yours." And with a gesture of dismissal, of tactical superiority, he turned his back to them and stepped smartly to the colonnade, ascended its steps, and resumed his watch, but with his head up and his bearing military.

"Are you all right?" the man asked her.

"Yes," she said. "I'm all right. But he hurt my arm."

"Do you need a doctor?"

"Oh no! No, it just hurts a little," she said quickly. She was looking at his face, which to her seemed impossibly smooth.

"Well, then," he said. "You'd better leave here, now," he said.

Very slowly, so slowly it would take them several minutes to get to the open gate, where his car was standing half in the street, the motor still running, she began to gather herself and to move, little by little—as slowly as she could, really. He was solicitous, he took her elbow once she seemed ready to move, but then he let her go at her own pace, and he accompanied her.

She had a lot of things inside her coat, he came to understand, and this affected how she moved as she managed her possessions, took inventory of them over and over, checking the pockets of the two overcoats she was wearing and God only knew how many other layers. The odor of her startled him—it was not what he expected a human being might smell like.

"What will you do, now?" the man said when they reached the gate. He was apparently anxious to get back into his car and be gone. "Is there someplace you can go?"

"I will go with you. All right," she said, as if agreeing reluctantly.

He was too surprised to speak, at first. She shuffled to the passenger door and he followed her there. "Look, I would like to help you. I could even take you somewhere else, if it's near here. But you can't come with me. I don't have any place for you."

She was looking into his car, which was very nice.

"I just don't," he said again. The authority he'd assumed unthinkingly against the doorman, clearly his inferior, had disappeared from his voice. Against her, who was not so clearly situated in relation to him in his usual ways of thinking about people, he must plead, not command.

"Look, we'll go to a take-out place two streets down and get you a cup of coffee and something to eat. But you'll have to take care of yourself from there on. All right?"

She was half-turned away from him, looking in through the closed window on the passenger's side.

"All right," he said, and he opened the door for her, and stood waiting, like her chauffeur. Slowly, almost afraid to catch her breath for fear of hexing the possibilities, she bent over a little and got into the car, one leg, then sitting, then the other, with his steadying hand at her trailing elbow.

He shut the car door after her. Inside, it smelled to her of an as yet unused world, it smelled of the sky, and she reached for the glove compartment knob and pressed it. The little hinged door swung down, and inside was a flashlight, a red plastic hand-mirror and some papers. She took out the mirror just as he was getting in.

"Please don't get into anything," he said, irritated. But he didn't dare to reach over and take his wife's mirror from her yet. "May I have that back?" he asked her politely. She was looking ahead, now, out the windshield, enchanted with the way the street looked.

"Ma'am?" he said. And he reached gently to take the mirror from her. When his fingers broke into her rapture she clutched the mirror to her breast and began to twist away from him. She found the door handle and opened the door quite readily, which surprised him, and got her legs out the door, so her back was to him, and she kept struggling, although he wasn't even touching her. Wearily he closed the glove compartment, letting her keep shifting and lurching by herself till she lunged out of the car and gained her feet and looked around her angrily.

The man got out, came around the car again, and said, "I'm sorry, you'll just have to get yourself wherever it is you're going." He reached for the mirror, once more, wondering by what tactic he might get it back. They both perceived voices behind them, through the open gate, on the colonnade, and they looked that way, thinking the owner might have come out to swear at the intruders he had been told of.

Into the doorman's hand something was being put by another man, also fairly young, bearded and wearing clothes much dirtier than the old woman's. He was carrying a white plastic shopping bag filled with things. They were talking loudly, the doorman was laughing, the other man had a troubled, frightened look on his face. But the doorman, after putting what was now in his hand into his coat pocket, ceremoniously opened the door of the shack, as if for a client, and the other man stooped to go in and shut it behind him.

How unfair this little tyrant had been. It had only needed the proper bribe to secure the place for the night. He must rent it out, the greedy son of a bitch. The man who had rescued her had robbed her of her chance to bargain for the place; and now he had gotten into his car and was driving off, and was gone.

Not one to linger on defeats or victories, perhaps, she turned away from the gate quickly, with resolve, and headed back down the street with a steady slow rolling stride, back toward where she had come from, where everybody was, the good and the bad. But the red mirror in her hands, held tight against her breasts, was putting a wild grin on her face.

STATE & WACKER

A man once lived . . . who found on the quay of Sligo a package containing three hundred pounds in notes. It was dropped by a foreign sea captain. This my man knew, but said nothing. It was money for freight . . .
   —W. B. Yeats, *The Celtic Twilight*

I

Gulls gliding round the lighthouse
that stands far out on a jetty
complain, complain nearby
over the river, sounding like
cats or a boy crying Ow!

2

In the subtropical nineteen-thirties
my young father and a young friend
buddied up to work as longshoremen
for a few dollars a day and lucky
to get it on the Houston Ship Channel,
till one hot Thursday morning
the friend was crushed by a bale,
five hundred pounds, of cotton
dropped on him for reasons men
believed at the time—loyalty this way,
loyalty that. And believe now.
The very next moment my father walked,
never returning for anything—
lunch, lunch bucket or pay.

Young men owning little, owing little
to anyone else, masters of nothing,
aiming not to be owned.

There was a boxer who could move
a bale of cotton an inch with one punch.

The Ship Channel stank of spilled crude oil,
rotted fruit, diesel fuel, dead fish,
and the one second it takes something
you don't wish to fall, to fail.
That too has a smell worth remembering.

3

Go north, now, go further back:
For longshoremen, for years,
historical hooves of horses and mules,
sonorous, everyday,
mythical, stopped
clopping on streets and
at the Chicago River drummed
loud on wharf planking.

Work boats—tenders, lighters—
loaded and offloaded barges,
long lines were dipped into deep schooners
wedged close at piers and riverside
docks. Ships converged where
there was freight, hauling lumber,
iron ore, wares, hemispheres;
ships going out carried steel,
grain, gravel, finished goods
and evils, all of this
is finished. Outbound and in
they floated, urged by wind
or with steam power walking
across the deep lake.

Peering into lightless warehouses,
into dank dim hatches, holding

a fistful of pale papers,
men called out, signaled
cranking cranes,
hooked crates and barrels and bales.
Heavy cargo creaked up, dangled down.
Stevedores working, stevedores looking.
Looking out.
Taking a stand. Standing clear.
Taking a break with a smoke.

4

Out on the lake, stack-plumes
and freighters inch along,
knowing or not knowing
what they reiterate. Or anchored
in harbor flocks, pleasure-sails
and silenced power growlers
rock like big guitars.
Songs for lifting and heaving and having
to labor rise only
in electric clubs at night.
Weightless dollar transactions
cross waters on the backs
of electrons and we too
in our bodies ride, rattling
toward work, cross.
In rain or sun (*How good*), over
the river bridges (*it is*),
inside tinny trains in debt
(*to be alive*). We peer down
through rusted trestles at
the backwards river that
does not remember.

ON BELMONT

Watch it, brother!—he said, who had come up beside me without my even noticing it as I was walking on crowded Belmont late one summer night. He had already dropped into a squat, half-leaning against a building wall, a brown-bagged bottle in one hand. Get down, he warned me.

Ragged, stoned, looking full of fear. I stopped near him.

I don't think I had heard even a backfire.

Machine guns, he said. I know, I was *there*, he said, turning his head from side to side.

Not machine guns, I said, to be helpful. Then I had what I thought was a good idea. I said, And even if it is, they're a long way from here. (They'd *have* to be, suppose it *was* possible, they were still blocks away from here, at least, off down the busy late-hours streets lit too bright. We had plenty of time.)

Oh, he said; meaning, Is that what you think? With a quick glance. His gaze sidelong, but strong. It would take too long to teach me. But he explained: That's when they're really bad, that's when they get you, when they're far away.

He stayed low, one knee half up, squatting on the other thigh, protecting the bottle held half behind him. He looked up and down the street. I waited as long as I could, maybe half a minute, but all this was over now, that was about as far as we could take it, now that we had had our moment of contact in this world, after the accumulated years when separately we had wandered other streets and other countries. We had happened to be momentarily side by side at the sound of whatever it had been, maybe a gun. I started on down Belmont, and got back my pace, I was heading for the train.

Maybe to him, still squatting and leaning there, not yet ready to stand up, or able, it seemed like he was the one who would get to where things made sense and were safe, and I was walking foolishly in a place of danger. How could he explain it to me, it was way too late for me and everybody like me.

CHRISTMAS

A typical hearing or trial in juvenile court, on the delinquency as opposed to the abuse-and-neglect side, is like a brief, routine dance. The public defenders work from a table to one side of the small courtroom, the state's attorneys from another at the other side. The clerk calls the next case. Someone official leaves the closed courtroom by the doors to the waiting area and, holding them open, calls out the minor respondent's name. Through another door to one side of the bench, a boy is brought in by a guard. A long moment later ("Someone is approaching, judge," says an attorney, to placate the impatient man behind the bench), into the courtroom from the waiting area come three women. The judge says, "Is mother here?" "Yes, judge," the public defender says, indicating one of the women. "And who is with mother?" the judge asks. "Grandmother and aunt," says the attorney. The judge says, "Aunt, please sit at the back of the courtroom," and the woman retreats without speaking. The other two wait, also silent.

Like the women who are here to stand with him, the child is black, this time. Everyone else in the courtroom is white. The boy's handcuffs were removed from his wrists at the side-door to the courtroom, and as instructed by the uniformed officer who accompanies him and stands behind him, the boy faces the center of the bench with his hands clasped behind his back and holding a light jacket, a tube of toothpaste and a toothbrush.

This legal episode takes three minutes. The state's attorney speaks; the judge speaks; the public defender speaks; the person of whom they are speaking is not asked to speak, and does not speak. Although they have had time, in their service, to learn somewhat the language that *he* speaks, they do not speak a language that is intelligible to *him*.

Something having been decided, he is taken out of the courtroom, the three women regroup and leave, talking about a Christmas present, and the clerk calls the next case. There are a lot of cases to be heard before the day is over, and the judge wants to deal with each one quickly.

The public defender gathers some papers, whispers for a few moments to one of his colleagues about another matter, while the next very short hearing or trial begins—whether to be postponed, broken off, or concluded—and then he goes out the same door through which his client was taken.

That door leads to a corridor. Along it are the chambers of seven or eight judges. At one end is a police desk. To one side of the raised police desk, where five or six officers are on duty, talking loudly among themselves, is the holding tank, a single large room with a glass wall facing the police desk, in which about fifty boys aged sixteen or younger are waiting— standing, talking, yelling, sitting, remaining silent, staring out through the glass wall and the glass door.

The public defender meets his client in a small bare windowless interview room. The client is fourteen years old and has been held for two weeks, so far, on a very serious charge. A violent crime. His hearing, which will take place in two more weeks, will determine whether he will be tried as a juvenile in this building and have some chance to go free again, after seven years, or will be sent to the court at 26th Street to be tried as an adult.

This boy is short, thin; he does not look directly at the public defender, his attorney, who is explaining to him what happened in the courtroom in those three minutes of the judge's time. It was decided that something will be decided. But this explanation, too, is in the language of courts. So in response to the explanation, which is that he is going to be given psychological tests, and he needs to be completely honest with the doctor, and then there will be another session before the judge, to determine where he will be tried, he says, "How long am I going to be in here?" For his crime, if he is convicted as an adult, he would be likely to remain in prison for most of the rest of his life, or all of it if his life is not long.

His attorney says, "That depends. But it's gonna be a while. We have to convince the judge not to send you to 26th Street, right?"

"Right."

"You know how we do that?"

"Oh, man." Exasperation and impatience.

"You know how we do that? You have to do two things—you have to not get written up for anything while you're here, and you have to do well in school, upstairs. Are you doing well in school, here?"

The child is not doing well. And he has already been written up once. People get in his face, he says. He says he has a temper. All he really wants to know is how long he will be in here.

"It could be a long time," his attorney says.

"*How* long? Am I going to get out for Christmas?"

"No."

"No?!" He doesn't believe this man is an attorney. He says he wants a *good* lawyer, he wants to pay five hundred dollars and have a *good* lawyer.

His sleeves are too long. His pants are too big. He shifts in his chair, again and again. The small brick-walled room doesn't fit him either. His jacket, toothbrush and toothpaste lie on the table.

Even in here, coming faintly from some corner, from behind one of these bricks, there are voices which—whether they're endangered or dangerous—are still free, on the street, still loud out there. That's the world he knows. He doesn't know any of all the other worlds. He and his friends are suspicious of other worlds. "Is it more important to you," the attorney says, "to react when someone is on you, so they *know* you won't tolerate that, *or* to spend the rest of your life in jail? If the judge hears that you got written up, he's gonna think that you're not taking this seriously, and if that's what he thinks, then he'll decide that you need to go to 26th Street. Right?"

The child fidgets violently in his chair and flings his arms to one side and then the other. He looks at every corner of the room and not at his attorney.

His attorney says, "Someone gets in your face, you have to walk away from it. Right? And in school, you need As and Bs. OK? That's so we can ask one of the teachers to come down to the courtroom and *tell* the judge that you should *not* be tried at 26th Street. Right?"

The inconclusive child is taken back into that part of the building that is behind locks. After he is gone, his attorney says of him, "He isn't going to make it. What he has to do is more than any adult could be reasonably expected to be able to do. And he's only fourteen."

The day proceeds. More trials, more hearings. The courthouse empties. All the different worlds, here and everywhere around here, go dark early at this time of year. After rush hour, whether at the happening street corners where traffic goes steadily by, slowly, or at the safe corners where nothing should occur, the snow falling since late afternoon is making everything quiet. And the street is bright in that strange, nighttime snow-lit way, with the light of a few street lamps, apartment and house lights, headlights, reflected up off the soft whiteness. Quiet.

And inside the holding tank, in the dining hall of the juvenile detention center, in the cells, noisy. People are getting in other people's faces. Taunting. Threatening. Losing control because threatened or taunted. Outside the dirty unbreakable windows, the snow is falling in the night, falling freely, softly, steadily.

CELEBRATION

The workday's over and
          three stools away from me
in the noisy bar-and-
          cheap-seafood-joint I want
to enjoy, a blind man—
          white hair, shabby good clothes,
a man led to what seems
          his customary place
by the young clear-eyed good-
          looking hostess—has lit
a half cigarette, drawn
          the drug in, is sipping
a draft beer, his lips smile;
          we wait; as I'm listening
to and writing down what,
          even if finally use-
less, I must try to think
          through after I transcribe
it from my small machine,
          the blind man, who can't know
what I'm doing, brings out
          of a pocket his own
recorder and in its
          ear whispers his own sound-
notes and I can't know what
          they are or what they're for.
Am I writing down the
          words that he is saying?

Amid loud talk and T
          V, clatter of service,
the sightful bartender
          brings each of us a bowl
of green-herbed memory
          and fish as intricate
in flavor as is thought

                    in echoes, places, grace-
notes, associations,
                    in recognitions and
repressions. Shaped in each
                    day's events, reshaped by
each day's wishes, wrongs, needs.
                    Our hunger feeds on wit-
ness, wants to sit down with
                    friends and allies. Even
while eating by myself
                    I feel a welcome I
had not expected, and
                    after he has his word
I want to give a friend
                    who works and comes here blind
from his hard good thought bread.

NO MATTER WHAT HAS HAPPENED THIS MAY

I love the little row of life along the low rusted garden-wire fence that divides my small city backyard from my neighbor's. The wild unruly rose, I hacked like a weed last spring; then it shot quick running lengths of vine in every direction and shuddered into a thickness of blown blossoms—the kind you can't cut and take because they fall apart—so I think I should cut it back as if to kill it again. The violets, just beautiful weeds. Then there are yellow-green horseradish leaves, they rose as fast as dandelions in today's rain and sun; and the oregano and mint are coming back, too, you can't discourage them. Last year's dry raspberry canes are leaning, caught in the soft thorns of the new, at the corner. And beyond them, the mostly gone magnolia in the widow's yard, behind ours, the white petals on the ground in a circle like a crocheted bedspread thrown down around the black trunk.

I went out to see what the end of the day was like, away from everything, for a minute, and it was drizzling slowly. I touched the ground, just to feel it wet against my palm; and the side of the house, too. It was quiet, and I saw two robins bringing weeds and twigs to a nesting place in the new leaves at the stumpy top of a trimmed buckeye limb. How little they need—weeds and some time—to build with.

In a month I may find a new one not yet fully fledged, lost from the nest, and put it on the highest limb I can reach, but not high enough to escape harm's way, I imagine, when the harm is a shock within it, a giving up already; and it will be dead before morning. That's happened before. But these robins were just building, and one came with a full beak and paused a moment on a lower branch and cocked its head and looked upward and shifted as if it were a muscled cat, of all things, about to leap, and then it did leap and disappeared into the clump of leaves, and shook them, as the single drops of rain were gently shaking them one by one, here and there.

I was getting wet but I felt held outside because I could hear, from inside the house, a woman and a child—my wife and my daughter—laughing in the bathtub together, their laughter not meant for me but brought out to me like a gift by the damp still air so I could see that like the rain and the robins and the row of weeds they too were working and building. I'm not going to mention, now, any harm or hurt they have suffered; no winter nor summer government; no green troops nor trimmed limbs of trees; no small figures beaten or fallen. I wiped the dirt off my palms and I picked up again the glass of wine I had carried out with me. I rejoiced. There was no way not to, wet with the sound of that laughter and whispering in the last light of a day we had lived.